Kat's Law

The Sawtooth Range

Samantha St. Claire

Kat's Law/Samantha St. Claire – 2nd ed.
ISBN 978-1-7327367-6-4

For Kat

The world is but a canvas to our imagination.
— HENRY DAVID THOREAU

CONTENTS

Her Father's Daughter

IDAHO TERRITORY 1888

DUST PARTICLES DANCED in a slender ray of sunlight streaming through an open window, before drifting down to rest on carefully organized shelves lined with apothecary jars. A young woman's fingers grasped one tall glass jar and removed it from the shelf. She narrowed her eyes to study the label and nodded before turning back to her patient.

"Are you sure we shouldn't wait for your father, Miss Kat?" Mr. Halverson, the father of the patient, asked.

Dr. Kathryn Meriwether closed her eyes, taking in a deep, steadying breath. Ignoring the question for the moment, she crossed the room to where a boy lay quietly on the examining table. Her flare of anger under control, she stepped around the boy's father to retrieve a bottle of iodine and cotton from the drawer.

In a voice she hoped conveyed her confidence, she answered him. "Mr. Halverson, I assure you that I am quite as capable of handling such an injury as my father."

She returned to the boy's side and began to clean the wound. His leg muscle tightened, causing her to glance up into his pale face. As much as she'd like to focus on the wound, she knew the boy needed comforting. "So, Jeremy, how old are you now? The last time I saw you, you couldn't have been much older than four or five. So, that must make you ten?" She knew he was younger, but the lie might provide a moment of distraction.

"No ma'am, I'm nine. My brother, William, he's ten." Jeremy clenched the sheet in his fists as she probed the wound. The momentary discomfort was worth it if she was able to thoroughly clean the laceration and prevent infection.

"That horse of yours really landed a good kick, didn't he, Jeremy?" She could see that the cut had gone deep, but she was confident that no nerves had been damaged.

The boy managed a crooked grin, piling up the freckles on one cheek. "Yes, ma'am. She's a caution. She knocked me clean over to the fence. For a while there I thought I'd been hit by lightning. My head hurt like blazes."

"Jeremy! Remember what your mother said about school yard language?"

"Sorry, Pa." The boy grimaced in response to his father's tone. "It hurt *real bad.*"

Kat turned her attention to the boy's head, seeing the beginnings of a bruise. "You hit the fence?" She touched the swollen tissue just above his left eye. It might be a more serious injury than the cut, she thought.

"Made me dizzy for quite a spell."

"Hmm." Kat lay her instruments to the boy's side. Stitching was easy. She rather liked it, taking pride in being recognized among her peers for the straightest stitches, leaving the smallest scars.

"You're sure, Miss Kat?" Kat turned again to face the boy's father. She pulled herself up to as tall as she could, but still only managed to raise her eyes to the man's chest. Five feet and two inches didn't give her a lot of elevation with which to work.

She smiled tightly at the man. "Mr. Halverson, it's 1888. Many women are entering the field of medicine. I've worked in a hospital where I've sewn up men who've been stabbed through to their backbone, and men impaled by steel girders. I've cleaned burned flesh from a dozen people injured in a factory explosion. We can wait for my father, and watch your son bleed, or you can trust me to do what I've been fully trained to do. You decide."

The man frowned and looked away from Kat's unflinching gaze. He tilted his head, took in a long thoughtful breath, before shoving his hands into his pockets. "Well, all right." Under his breath he added, "I guess a woman's pretty good at sewing after all."

Kat could feel the blood rising to her cheeks, so she worked to check a bitter retort. Instead she turned back to the table and smiled sweetly at the boy. "Jeremy, just imagine that I'm going to put a hem in your leg." She patted his good leg, picking up the needle. It *was* a bit like the needlework she'd seen her mother do often enough, but something she'd never bothered with as a girl. She'd found far more satisfaction in stitching together torn flesh.

Jeremy grinned down at her from the narrow wagon bench while Mr. Halverson stood awkwardly on the porch, his hat gripped tightly in his hand. "Thanks, Miss Kat."

"You're welcome, Mr. Halverson." Kat assumed some responsibility for his discomfort, and tried to assuage her guilt by adapting a less professional tone of voice. "Please remember what I told you about watching Jeremy for the next few hours. He shouldn't do any chores for a day or so, just in case. Head traumas are nothing to ignore." She rubbed her hands on her apron, wincing as she did. Her hands had become painfully dry and cracked from washing them so often in the hospital.

"Will do. It's good to have you back." He put his hat back on his head and climbed into the wagon next to his son. "My Josephina sure missed you when you left for school. She's going to be mighty glad to see you."

A laughing image of her childhood friend, pig tails swinging, flashed into her mind. Next to her father, she missed Josie most of all. "I can honestly say that my first year away there was not a day that passed that I didn't think about her. It's been hard to imagine her as a married woman with children. She must have her hands full if they're half as precocious as she was when we were growing up."

"Oh, to be sure! You two have a lot to catch up on. You planning to stay for a while? Know your dad would be a happy man if you did. He's been pretty lonely since your ma passed away."

She'd heard the question at least a dozen times in the past three days. Drawing her shoulders back and folding her hands at her waist, she looked past the man down the hill to the patchwork of houses and small businesses that comprised the settlement of Snowberry, in Idaho Territory. "Well, Mr. Halverson, since I just arrived, I suppose I'll be here awhile. Please tell Josie I'll be out to see her soon if she doesn't make it to town before I do." She laughed lightly, remembering that her father had told her Josie was eight months pregnant.

He tipped his hat. "Will do. Give my regards to the doc, Miss Kat."

"Actually, it's Dr. Meriwether now." Kat put on her most disarming smile, determined to make her point without provoking offense. She'd keep reminding them until they got it right. She'd worked too hard, endured too much, for the right to be called by that title.

Mr. Halverson's brow formed a neat 'v' before his eyes widened with understanding. "Oh yeah!" He clucked to the mule and pulled away. "Imagine that!"

Kat stood on the porch, her hand resting lightly on its faded blue railing, watching them drive the short distance down from the bench and on into the main street, muddy with spring rains. So much remained as it always had. So much had changed, like her. Some things would have to change after four years. She'd prepared herself for them, but was still surprised by those she'd not anticipated, like the growth of the valley. Idaho Territory was rapidly filling up with settlers, miners, and business men. The long valley that stretched out for thirty miles along the Payette River would soon be lined with small settlements like this one. She speculated, as many others, that it would not be long before the territory, that had provided a pathway to the travelers of the Oregon Trail, would earn statehood.

She reached into the pocket of her skirt and pulled out the letter, wrinkled and smudged from having been read so many times in the past two weeks. The letter was more than an invitation, it was a door to everything she'd wanted since entering medical school, an opportunity to work in a new hospital with educated men and women, now her equals.

A cloud passed over her face, causing the corners of her mouth to turn down.

She lifted her gaze to the town again, where a one-horse buggy plodded its way up the hill to the bench. Oh, how she'd missed seeing him come up that road after visiting patients all day. His return signaled the end of the day and the time when he belonged to her alone. As much as she'd missed Josie, leaving her father had plunged her into a period of grief that had nearly derailed her dream. Only by burying herself in her studies was she able to pull herself through those first lonely months. Instead of crying herself to sleep, she would study until her eyes grew too heavy to hold open.

Many were the mornings she awoke with her face creased by the edges of the book that had become her pillow. She shivered at the memory.

She looked down at the letter still in her hand. As much as her dream was about to come true with this invitation, his would surely die. Carefully folding the letter, she pushed it deep into her pocket. Looking back to the road, she saw her father's hand lift as he hailed her. At the familiar sight, a thrill filled her as her childhood memories came rushing back. Lifting her skirt to her ankles, she gave into the little girl habit and trotted down the road to greet him.

Chapter 2

Once a Ranger

WAS IT THE GIRL'S choking scream or the vision of the blood-soaked snow that woke him this time? He sat on the edge of his bed with elbows to knees, palms pressed tightly to his closed eyes. It didn't matter anymore. The dream was always the same, ending the same, and he always awoke like this, sweat drenched shirt, breathing like he'd run for miles. He *had* been running, for months now, from the dream, from the memory that wouldn't leave him. Not even here, 1,500 miles away, could he escape it.

Jonathan Winthrop leaned further forward, pressing the palms harder into his eyes until he felt pain. That was real. How much of the dream was based in reality? Once again, he wished that he could sleep, just one night, without the haunting.

Rising wearily to his feet, he crossed the wood floor to the crude table bravely supporting a bucket of water. Splashing cold water on his face helped to clear his head. Despite the chill of the morning, he stripped off his shirt and doused his body with cold spring water. He shivered. Taking the small mirror and propping it on the window sill, he did what he'd done for years as a Texas Ranger. He shaved. It didn't matter the weather, snow or heat. It didn't matter the place, prosperous town or high desert. He took the time to groom himself, to shave and attend to the neatness of his clothing. He was a Texas Ranger, a title worthy of respect.

Gazing in the mirror, he hesitated, the razor lifted half-way to his cheek. But he wasn't a Ranger now, was he? And respect? He'd none for himself, why would others give it to him? But habits die hard so he touched the razor to his cheek and drew it up against the night's growth of stubble. The routine slowed his breathing, forcing the dream back into that dark haunted corner of his mind where it would wait until he closed his eyes to sleep.

Rummaging through the drawer, he pulled out a clean shirt and slipped it on. After looking in the mirror again, he touched his temple where strands of gray hair peppered through brown. This was something he'd only noticed since the dreams began.

"Jonathan, you're turning into an old man, and old men don't make their living with a gun." He said it aloud, and felt a little better for it. Sometimes a little lie to oneself can help, but only for a little while. The *need* to find another line of work had nothing to do with a lessening of his skills and everything to do with shattered confidence.

Rays of brilliant gold, over-laid with pink spilled over the eastern mountain range as he stepped from the bunkhouse into a crisp spring Idaho morning. The chill drove away the nightmare's last echoes, pulling him back into the present. He breathed deep taking in the fragrant incense of pine and cedar. The climate and the landscape were vastly different from his native Texas, a difference he rather favored.

His mare nickered a greeting, impatient for breakfast. He called to her, "What are you whining about? You never used to wake up in a dry bed. You're growing spoiled. Count your blessings, girl!"

The bay called again, more persistent this time. Jonathan stepped down from the porch and crossed the muddy yard to her corral. She loved scratches almost as much as grain, at least that's what Jonathan supposed from her insistent nudging. He obliged, as her neck extended, eye lids lowered in pleasure.

After several minutes of indulging her, he said, "Okay, enough of that." Jonathan threw her breakfast into the corral and waited awhile to watch her nuzzle through the grass in search of grain. He knew he loved that mare too much, but more than anyone in his life in recent years, she'd been his faithful friend. Conversations with her were short and to the point, and never unduly emotional even if she was a mare. With her, there was never the confusion of ambiguous language or awkward silence.

"Mr. Winthrop!" A gangly boy of thirteen, all legs and arms not yet grown into, flapped at him from the porch of the main house. The house was just a larger shack really, but this one, unlike the bunkhouse, held a fireplace and facilities for cooking.

"Father's got breakfast ready," he shouted, scaring a hen into a frantic dash across the yard.

Jonathan waved back. "Thanks, Adam. Be there in a minute."

He combed his fingers through his mop of wavy brown hair and pushed his hat low on his brow. The mare looked up and snorted.

"Don't talk with your mouth full," Jonathan threw back and strode across the yard, his long legs stepping effortlessly across a dozen puddles along the way.

Timothy Hindricks wasn't much of a rancher, *yet*. But Jonathan considered himself mighty lucky to have met up with a man who knew how to cook. Opening the door to the enticing smell of fried ham and biscuits was nearly akin to heaven as far as he was concerned. A dozen years on the trail and more in the war had nearly brought him to despair of ever eating anything that didn't taste like rawhide or burnt flour. It seemed everything he'd eaten in those years had been drained of every ounce of moisture, requiring a canteen of water to even wash it all down. He wondered at times if his own saddle would have had more to offer in terms of flavor.

But Timothy! Well, Jonathan was convinced Timothy knew magic when it came to cooking, and with nearly every meal Jonathan could count on a pitcher of gravy to pour over everything. And he did. Timothy was a man who could cook, and as his appearance attested to, he liked to eat his own cooking nearly as much.

As Jonathan stepped through the door, Timothy rubbed his hands on the apron around his generous girth, greeting him as he did. "Good morning, Jon! Splendid morning, don't you think? Sky the color of the blush on a pretty girl's cheek!"

Jonathan had never met a man with such enthusiasm for the ordinary. But then, he'd never befriended a school teacher. The ones he'd known growing up in east Texas seemed more inclined to display their enthusiasm for discipline and he'd known that enthusiasm often enough on the seat of his britches. Taking the mug of hot coffee from Adam's hand, he considered Timothy's word picture. It had been colorful, but he might have likened it to the color of his hands after washing them in a cold mountain stream. He chuckled to himself. He'd certainly never be a poet.

Timothy dished up a generous helping of ham and placed it on the table next to a stack of books with titles such as *Cattle: Their Breeds, Management, and Diseases* and *The Hearty Devon Breed*.

"Adam and I already had ours. You take your time." He picked up a bowl of gravy and pushed it across the table. "Been wanting to talk to you about our agreement." Timothy lowered himself onto a stool across from Jonathan.

Jonathan looked up, an eyebrow cocked expectantly. "Sounds a mite ominous the way you put it, Timothy."

Timothy threw back his head and laughed. "No, nothing bad. Not at all. Much to the contrary." He picked up a spoon and held it by the handle, turning the tip of its bowl in circles on the tablecloth.

Jonathan grew more curious at the man's hesitancy. He leaned back in the chair and studied Timothy's suddenly serious face. "Well?"

Timothy shifted and he chewed on his lip for a few moments before answering. "I know that you didn't much like the idea of baby-sitting two greenhorns like Adam and I, especially such a long way across the country. We'd never have made it without you." His face grew quiet as he met Jonathan's steady gaze. "Fact is, we'd not only have had our cattle stolen, but we'd likely be dead now."

Adam brought his father a steaming mug of coffee and sat at the table.

"Thanks, son."

"You held your own, both you and Adam." Jonathan sipped tentatively at his coffee, and then took a longer drink after judging its heat.

"That's generous of you. I may be foolish at times, like attempting to start this ranch with no more experience than what I've gleaned from books, but I'm no fool. Those three men we met north of Salt Lake had no good intentions when they asked to sign on and help us with the cattle. You knew that."

Jonathan shrugged his shoulder and leaned forward, resting his elbows easily on the table. He was a good judge of character. He'd learned that from years of tracking down men gone bad from greed and stupidity. And Timothy was right, those three men had venom in their blood, as bad as they come. But Timothy was a trusting man and he just hadn't seen it, hiring the men against Jonathan's advice to the contrary.

"So, what's your point? We made it through. This is a fine piece of land you found, and you have enough stock left to establish yourself as a rancher." He winked at Adam. "And Adam, here, well. . .he's shown he's made from strong stock himself."

Adam cast his eyes to the table, color rising to his cheeks at the compliment.

Timothy nodded. "You're right. And I know we agreed that you would only stay through the winter, but. . ." He glanced over at Adam before continuing. "Well, Adam and I would like you to stay on."

Jonathan sat back, his face an expressionless mask.

"Really, Jonathan, why not? There's that parcel down by the river between here and the North Fork. It's a nice piece of land and plenty of range for your own herd." He was talking fast now. "If you like, we'll cut out half the herd come summer. You've got the summer months to build yourself a snug little cabin near the stream that feeds into the river. We'll be neighbors!" Timothy's voice had raised a pitch.

Jonathan remained stoic.

"Where else do you have to be?" It was Adam who spoke. When Jonathan turned his attention to him, Adam said, "Isn't this as good a place as any to settle down?"

Jonathan gave the boy a thin smile. "Who said I wanted to settle down?"

There was a long silence, broken only by Jonathan as he took another long drink of coffee. Jonathan saw the boy's shoulders sag. The boy was so young, and probably more suited to the study of those books in the boxes his father had insisted on toting with them. He just didn't seem cut out for frontier life from Jonathan's perspective. But he also knew the boy was devoted to his father, and by extension, his father's dream.

"Look, Timothy, I appreciate your offer, but I'm no cattleman. I told you that." He put his cup down and spread his hands on the table while he considered what Timothy was asking and offering. "I'll do this. I'll stay through the summer."

Timothy grinned at Jonathan. "I appreciate it. We both do."

Jonathan picked up his fork and stabbed at a slice of ham. It was a concession that didn't cost him anything but time, and he knew the boy was right. Where else did he have to be? Besides the cooking was mighty fine.

Adam left the cabin to start his chores. Timothy remained at the table and watched Jonathan for a short time before asking, "But will you at least consider staying on? You're a good man, and I think the boy can learn a lot from you. I can teach him Latin, mathematics, and the classics, but I can't teach him how to be what you are."

Jonathan continued chewing, with the air of a man more interested in digesting words than ham. He picked up his cup and took a slow drink hoping the warm coffee would make the bite wash down more easily. At last he looked up and asked, "And what do you think I am?"

Timothy leaned forward. "You're a man of integrity. You're strong and self-confident. You're everything a man needs to be in a country like this."

Jonathan gripped the fork handle until he felt it begin to bend in his hand. Perhaps that was who he had been, once upon a time. But now?

Chapter 3

Disciplines of Restraint

NATHANIEL MERIWETHER CHEWED with interest the vaguely familiar substance he'd willingly placed into his mouth. He was aware that he needed to swallow it, but was reluctant to do so. He was also keenly aware of his daughter, Kat, watching him with the intensity of a falcon. A man known for supreme self-control, he worked the muscles of his throat and managed to swallow. At the same time, he reached rather rapidly for his coffee and swallowing it successfully moved the last stubborn bits down his throat. He might have fooled anyone else, but not Kat, never Kat.

Kat lifted the biscuit to her open lips and stopped. She studied it for a moment then lifted her eyes to meet her father's placid expression.

"Papa, you are one of the bravest men I've ever known. This is awful!"

Nathaniel dropped his gaze to the half-eaten biscuit, scorched eggs, and wedge of shoe leather still on his plate that had once been from some fine juicy hog. He picked up the last of the biscuit and tossed it in his mouth, chewing with enthusiasm. He mumbled, "I have no idea what you're talking about. This is great!"

She watched him chew for a full minute. "You're also one of the worst liars."

Nathaniel choked, a combined result of the dry biscuit awkwardly lodged in his throat and the laughter he could no longer control. He reached for his coffee again.

Kat covered her mouth with her napkin and laughed. Tears were streaming down her face before she could manage to say anything. "I'm so sorry. I really wanted to make you something special. I should have let you cook. You always were better than I was in the kitchen."

"Nonsense! The coffee is magnificent!" He patted her hand and chuckled.

Kat shook her head, then rose to her feet and threw her arms around her father's neck. "I've missed you so much, Papa!"

He pulled her down to sit on his knee. "I've missed you too, honey." Pushing a lock of hair from her face, he said, "You know, when I picked you up from the stage station, I hardly recognized you. You were dressed so grand and looked so poised, so stylish and grown up. But then you saw me and smiled. Your eyes crinkled the way your mother's did when she would tease me, and I knew my little girl had come home." He patted her arm. "I'd feared some young doctor would have snatched you up while you were in Boston and I'd not see you again."

Kat frowned and punched him playfully. "Papa, how could you think that?"

"Because it's only natural. Because you are a pretty young woman, smart, funny, and quite a catch!" He touched the tip of her nose. "Cute as a button."

Kat hugged his neck again. "You've always been a romantic. Besides, didn't I tell you I wouldn't let any-one, even if he were as handsome as you," she touched his nose, "keep me from finishing school?"

"And you didn't, did you?" There was a tone in his voice of something she couldn't quite identify, melan-choly perhaps.

"No!" Kat stood and smoothed her skirt before be-ginning to clear the table.

Nathaniel took her hand in his, staring up into her brown eyes, so much like her mother's. The shocking resemblance made him falter. "You know how proud I am of you, don't you?"

She put her hand over his, her face softening. "Yes, Papa. I know."

"I wish I could have been there when they gave you your honors. I really do."

"Papa, please, you don't need to explain. I know what your life here is like. Haven't I spent most of my life right here watching you caring for everyone in this town? They could ill afford to have you leave for even as much as a day, let alone the weeks it might have taken."

She knelt down beside his chair, still holding his hand. "Besides, you *were* there. You've been with me these past six years, every day. When I was studying a textbook and I read about the proper way to set a fracture, I could hear your voice telling me how to do it. Because you were my first teacher. I learned so much from you before I even walked through the door of the school, or heard my first lecture, or performed my first autopsy. Dr. Nathaniel Meriwether made me the doctor I am today."

Nathaniel leaned forward and brushed her forehead with his lips.

"Now go put on your town clothes and I'll take you to Mrs. Halverson's boarding house for some breakfast."

He looked at her with mock severity. "You really are an awful cook."

She realized that she should have left the hat at home two minutes after walking into the mercantile and catching the stares of two women she didn't know. This was Snowberry, not Boston.

"Kat!" The voice came from the back of the store, where a cheerful, middle-aged woman stepped from behind the counter. Her arms opened wide as she crossed the room. "I was wondering when you'd get around to visiting me!"

Kat stepped forward, allowing the older woman to pull her into an embrace. "Mrs. Forester, I've missed you." She immediately forgot about her discomfort in the presence of her father's oldest friend in Snowberry, a woman who'd done her best to keep Kat from turning into a complete tomboy. Somehow. she'd managed to persuade not only her father but Kat herself to wear a proper dress on the first day of school, a dress she'd sewn for her.

Amy Forester stepped back, still holding Kat's hands and looked her up and down with an appraising eye. She beamed at her. "You're quite the stylish lady now! So pretty. No one would know how much of a fuss you put up about skirts and petticoats when you were a girl."

Mrs. Forester dropped Kat's hands and took another step back one hand holding her chin. "Spin around for me."

Kat, feeling foolish, spun once. She was hardly dressed to current styles fashionable in the East, not even wearing a bustle to enhance her figure.

"So, this is the latest fashion I suppose. I knew that hoops were no longer being worn." She tipped back her head. "Sure am glad for that! I can't imagine any woman came up with that idea, can you?"

Kat felt the movement of air and rush of cold as the door opened behind her. Before turning, she noted the straightening of posture and sudden altering of expression in the faces of the three other women in the store. Kat turned to see a young man, slender, the cut of his clothing suggesting he was either himself or connected to someone with substantial means. She discerned this in an instance, but what arrested her attention for a second longer were his eyes, a shade of blue she'd never imagined God would have given to any human. They were unusually pale, like a mid-day sky in the height of an Idaho summer. She tugged at her ear and returned her attention to her friend.

"Mrs. Forester, are you still sewing for those unfortunates like myself without the skill? I had a skirt I was hoping you could help me to alter."

"Why yes, Kat. I'm still at it." Mrs. Forester stepped behind the counter again. "I'd love to help."

"That's wonderful," Kat said as she turned to the door again. "I'll bring it by later. Maybe I can catch you when you aren't as busy."

"That sounds fine. I'll look forward to a longer visit. We can have a cup of tea and I'll catch you up on all the town gossip." She winked and resumed her conversation with her customers.

Kat took a step and ran head on into the man who seemed to have intentionally placed himself into her path. "Pardon me!" he said as he raised his hat.

Kat stepped back. "No, I'm sure I wasn't looking where I was going." She stepped to the side. "Excuse me."

He backed up and leaned forward to peer at her beneath the cover of her hat as he asked, "You're new here, aren't you?"

"Not really. I was born and raised here, actually. I've just returned after being away for a while." She took another step to the door. He followed.

"Oh, you must be Dr. Meriwether's daughter! Well, please let me introduce myself." He made a slight bow of his head. "My name's Ethan. Ethan Hall."

Kat dipped her head and extended her gloved hand. She instantly wished she'd left the gloves at home as well as the hat, thinking how pretentious she must appear. "Dr. Kathryn Meriwether."

Ethan took her hand in his, and bowed his head again. "*Very* pleased to meet you, *Dr.* Meriwether."

She realized that this was the first time anyone in Snowberry had called her that. She felt a warm rush of blood to her face, not able to hide the pleasure his response had given her.

"Are we going to be seeing more of you here? I mean are you staying for a while?" His mouth curved into a slow smile, revealing straight white teeth. "It would be a pleasure to get to know you. The town's growing now with the new silver strike near the Salmon River to the north. We may have need of your services. Doctors are scarce out here, worth their own weight in gold."

There was something about his easy smile she found disturbing, but those startling eyes intrigued her. She broke off her study of the man, then realized that he was still holding her hand. As graciously as she could without leaving her glove in his hand, she withdrew from his grasp. "Well, I would suppose my father can continue to care for the needs of the town. He's been doing it for a very long while."

Even as she said it, she felt the quiver of doubt, doubt that had begun when the wagon she'd arrived in had crested the hill, beginning its descent into the valley. Surprisingly, the valley floor had become a network of streets with twice the houses and businesses than had comprised the town she had left. It would be a lot for one doctor to handle such a fast-growing community.

Ethan took her elbow, accompanying her to the door. "Well, whether you stay or not, I think my father and I should have you and your father join us for dinner. The new boarding house serves a very respectable dinner, even for someone with refined tastes, such as you must have developed in the East. Boston wasn't it?"

She nodded. He'd certainly done his homework.

Ethan straightened, pulling himself to his full height. At five feet two inches, Kat's head barely reached his shoulder. He was an impressive specimen she decided, appraising him with what she told herself was a doctor's eye. Blond hair, mid-twenties perhaps, certainly not more than 30, long muscular arms and legs, broad shoulders, narrow waist. She tugged on her ear, wincing as she did, reminding herself that such distractions were not for her at this time in her life. Nodding to him, she strode past him with quick steps to the door, her skirt sweeping against his leg as she passed.

Ethan called after her, "It was nice to have met you. I'm certain we'll be seeing each other again."

She turned back at the door. "Yes, Mr. Hall. That's very possible. It's still a small town." She lifted her hand waving to her friend. "Goodbye, Mrs. Forester! I'll see you soon."

Her eyes hesitated for only a second as she turned again, arrested by those ghostly eyes. Yes - a fine specimen indeed. And as she stepped through the door she laughed to herself. *A fine specimen for someone else, not you, Dr. Meriwether. He's the kind that would insist you give up everything you've worked for to have his babies and cook him burned biscuits every morning. And odds are in favor of him one day turning those baby blues on someone younger and more gullible than you!*

Unpleasant Changes

KAT SAT BOLT upright throwing off the quilt, her eyes attempting to focus in the sliver of moonlight that streamed through her window. It took her awhile to remember where she was, then to work out the puzzle of what had awakened her.

"Doc! Doc! Open the door! We need you!" The voice was followed by another pounding on the front door, more insistent this time.

Throwing on her dressing gown, she made it to the door of the office before her father emerged bleary eyed from his own bedroom. She opened the door to a gush of chilling wind and was nearly knocked over by the two men who squeezed through the doorframe, stumbling into the room. One was obviously hurt, a trail of blood leaving a crimson streak on the floor.

Kat lit a lamp and led them into the examining room where she hung the lamp over the table. The injured man was not conscious, and judging from the look of his stained clothing, he'd already lost a considerable amount of blood.

"Hello Gabe, who'd you bring me?" Nathaniel asked the question in that same exaggerated slowness of speech that Kat had heard him adapt whenever he was faced with a medical case. He'd told her years ago it was his way of slowing his mind to take in the whole picture, not just the injury or the fever. If he didn't, he'd told her, I can miss some important details, a secondary wound that might even be more life-threatening, or an infected cut on a foot that might be the cause of the fever. It was that same thinking that had caused her to examine the boy's head as well as the cut from the horse's hoof. But sometimes his intentionally slow approach to a crisis, unnerved her - like now.

"He's the wagon driver from the silver fields, Zack Clark." The man's voice was husky, and Kat assumed from his obvious concern that he knew the injured man well.

"We found him when we went searching after the wagon was late arriving at Smith's Ferry. He was just lying there in the road where they left him. The wagon with the cash box was taken, and they just left him there to bleed to death." Kat could see the man's simmering rage contort his face.

"The guard's gone. Don't know if he was part of it or not. Name was Tom, new man." Gabe rubbed a bloody hand across his face after he and Nathaniel lifted his friend onto the table.

Her father had pulled on his apron, already cutting the man's clothing from the wound. He spoke to Gabe as he did. "Why don't you make yourself some coffee and go sit down in the kitchen. You look worn out."

Kat hadn't wasted time and in those few minutes had started water boiling on the cook stove and was now gathering the necessary instruments from her father's cabinets. She stepped to his side with a tray containing an assortment. She watched him, keeping her tongue, while he concentrated on his examination.

Nathaniel spoke while he worked. "Looks like the bullet went clear through. That's good. I can't see any damage to the vital organs." He stepped aside, nodding to Kat. "What do you think?"

She leaned in, but in the dim light it was difficult to determine if her father was correct. Picking up a second lamp, she handed it to her father. "Here, Papa, hold this for me." It was hard not to compare the poor facilities her father had to work with against those of the modern hospital she'd just left. Surgeries there were well lit, most even had replaced gas lights with Mr. Edison's amazing electric bulbs. What a difference!

Again, she bent over the man's chest, probing gently. Assuming that he was beyond feeling any further discomfort, she used the scalpel to cut a small incision effectively widening the point of the bullet entry. "Closer, Papa."

Nathaniel moved the light to above her shoulder. Gently she pulled the tissue away from the wound.

"I think there must be something else going on. We need to take a look before we stitch this closed, don't you agree?" Kat glanced up at her father.

Nathaniel stepped closer, handing the lamp to Kat. He frowned. "I think you may be right. Couldn't see it. Think there's some foreign matter there, could be a portion of his shirt."

Kat quickly retrieved the bottle of carbolic acid and clean cloths from the shelf. She scowled as she soaked the cloth. As thoroughly as she could, she applied it around the wound and a good deal beyond. If only her father had access to a machine like the one they had used in the hospital to cleanse the entire area. She shivered at the memory of the lectures she'd heard about the results of primitive frontier operations without such modern equipment. As much as her father kept up with modern treatments through journals and newly published books, he could ill afford the equipment common now in eastern practices. At least he could begin to stock some of the more recent vaccines. But that was a topic for later discussion.

A small bone fragment and piece of the man's shirt was removed from the man's chest before Nathaniel asked Kat to close the wound. She knew her father took pride in his record as a physician. His surgeries were clean.

Kat touched Gabe's knee, causing the weary man to wake with a start. "We think your friend is going to be all right."

The man looked at Nathaniel for confirmation. "You sure?"

"No, Gabe, I'm not."

Kat looked up sharply. That wasn't the kind of response she'd been taught to give at the hospital.

Nathaniel smiled as he placed his hand on Gabe's shoulder. "But I think he has a very good chance."

"Thanks, Doc." Gabe stood and entered the surgery to see for himself that his friend was still breathing.

"You know, you can thank my daughter as well, the other Dr. Meriwether. She saw something I missed."

"No, Dr. Meriwether," Kat said. "I'm confident you would have found it."

Her father gave her a weary smile. "Modesty doesn't marry well to medicine, Doctor."

Gabe's face grew dark, his brows lowered over eyes that had become narrow slits. "We gotta find a way to stop these robberies! This is the third time they've hit the wagon. That posse the sheriff has put together don't do a spit of good." He slapped his leg with his hat, causing a cloud of dust to sift about him.

"The town has a sheriff? When did we have to hire a sheriff? We've never had that kind of trouble." Kat's face reflected her surprise and disapproval.

"The town is growing, hon. We've had more trouble since the silver strike in the mountains north above the Salmon," Nathaniel explained. "But I have to agree with you. They haven't managed to catch anyone."

"Hall and his posse ain't worth the nickel in them badges they wear," Gabe spat back. "All that switching trails from one side of the mountain to the other, hasn't done a lick of good."

Kat remembered the pale-eyed Hall she'd met that morning. Surely, he wasn't the one they spoke of. "Are you talking about Ethan Hall?"

Nathaniel looked at Kat in surprise. "You know him?"

"I . . . bumped into him today at the store," she said.

"Well, he's not the sheriff, but he's his son and part of the so-called posse. The sheriff is Gilford Hall."

Gabe slammed his hat on his head and opened the door, but stopped in the doorway, turned and tipped his hat to Kat. "Thanks, Dr. Meriwether."

"You're welcome. We'll let you know when your friend is out of the woods." She closed the door behind him and turned to her father.

"So, when did the town hire a sheriff, Papa? When did all this trouble start?"

Nathaniel walked to the stove, poured a cup of tepid coffee and handed it to Kat. She shook her head, still puzzling over this new revelation.

He took a sip, wrinkling his nose as he did. "Gilford Hall came to town about a year ago, right after the silver discovery." Pulling back a chair, he sat heavily, running fingers through his tangled gray hair.

"So, was he elected or hired from somewhere else?" Kat asked.

"No, nothing that formal. He's really more like a vigilante in my opinion, who just calls himself sheriff. But when the robberies started, well people around here just let him be.

It started with robberies in the camps up north. Then it spread to the wagon attacks."

"So, what else does he do here? Does he run a store? A ranch? Surely, there isn't enough criminal activity here to keep him busy," Kat asked.

Nathaniel shook his head. "No. But he built himself a very nice house up in the foothills north of town."

Kat scowled. "I don't like it!"

"You aren't alone in that." He downed the rest of his coffee, rising stiffly to his feet. He seemed reluctant to discuss it any further, whether from fatigue or frustration, she didn't know.

"I'm going back to bed. You going to sit with our patient while I catch a few hours of sleep?"

"Sure, Papa."

Before turning to his room, he leaned over and kissed her cheek. "Things have changed a bit." He gave her a weary smile. "See you in the morning."

Pulling a blanket from her bed, she made a comfortable nest by the wood stove where she could watch over her patient through the open door. She pulled the blanket tight around her shoulders, opening the book she'd been trying to read for the past week. After reading the same paragraph for the fifth time, still not aware of who had done what to who, she put it aside.

She pulled her knees close to her chest, wrapping her arms about them.

What was happening to her little town of Snowberry? Whatever it was, she wasn't pleased to see it changing the town she'd held close to her heart these past years. She was pleased with the signs of growth and prosperity. But the violence, well that just wasn't acceptable!

Chapter 5

A Deer in the Crosshairs

IT WASN'T THAT she couldn't get up. It was an issue of how to accomplish it while maintaining some remnant of dignity. The length of her skirt, the heel of her boot, even the mud had all contrived cruelly against her. As a result, she found herself sitting in a stinking, sopping mud hole on the very public corner of Main and 3rd Street.

She pushed a lock of errant hair from her face, managing not only to smear mud on her hair but on her cheek as well. "Lovely! Just lovely!" she muttered.

"Dr. Meriwether, may I assist you?"

She took the proffered hand as an unquestioned means of salvation from her ever-deepening morass. However, she regretted her blind acceptance when she finally regained her feet to look up into the face of her unlooked for savior. As far as faces, Ethan Hall's wasn't hard to look at. But after learning of his family's self-appointment as law keepers combined with his ingratiating air, made it difficult for her to be gracious. But gracious was what she must be. Etiquette aside, she *was* grateful.

He retrieved her soiled package, holding it as it dripped, in his outstretched hand. "I think this is yours."

She took it, holding it away from her like a dead rodent. "Thank you," she said curtly.

"May I assist you to the walkway? It's very slippery here." As he took her arm and steered her through the mud and up the two steps to the boardwalk, she squashed down a quip about the obviousness of his observation. To make matters worse, she slipped *again* as they reached the relative stability of the boardwalk, the inch-thick layer of mud caked on her boots sending her flailing for the handrail. Infuriatingly smug, he took a firm grip on her elbow to steady her.

Kat granted him a strictly measured half smile. "Thank you."

Ethan looked down at her shoes, stating matter-of-factly, "You'll not get far like that." Quickly stepping off the walkway, he picked up a splintered stick of kindling from the side of the building. "Here, lean on my back and let me scrape off the worst of this."

He bent down, lifting not only her foot but the hem of her petticoat. Kat looked straight ahead, mortified. She was like a horse having its hooves picked. Blood rose to her face, but with one foot held in the air she was no more able to move away than the horse would have. So, she took a deep breath, struggling to remember how she'd managed to get through a number of awkward, unpleasant experiences as one of only three women in her class at medical school. She mentally detached herself from her body. It had become an effective behavior management technique. Regrettably, the removed perspective of her mortifying predicament only made her feel more ridiculous.

Ethan put down her foot and tapped her other leg. Kat looked down at him, a heated remonstration sizzling just on the tip of her tongue. She stopped herself. Oh yes, just like a horse she would need to raise the second foot. She inhaled another deep breath and straightened her shoulders to find herself looking into the amused face of a very tall man, so opposite in appearance from Ethan as to be startling. Whereas Ethan's fair complexion and pale eyes made him classically beautiful, this man was dark and ruggedly attractive. He tipped his hat courteously, exposing a line of tan that left his forehead pale. He nodded to her, and she distinctly saw that his mouth twitched, a smile tugging at the corners. "Good morning, ma'am."

She pulled her chin up an inch, managing to lose her balance in the movement. The newcomer caught her elbow. Kat grabbed at his arm to stabilize herself and dropped the package yet again.

Ethan dropped her foot to the wooden step quite abruptly. Both he and the stranger reached for the package at the same moment. Their eyes met in a silent battle of wills. Ethan jerked the package out of the other man's hand.

Ethan made a feeble attempt to shake off the layer of mud on the package before handing it to Kat. "Here you are, Dr. Meriwether. Hope it isn't breakable."

She managed another thin smile. What was it about him that disturbed her? "Mr. Hall, you seem to be quite...helpful. Thank you." She tested her footing before taking a step.

Ethan made a small bow while tipping his hat. "Anytime, Dr. Meriwether. Anytime." Kat felt relieved to see him walk away in the opposite direction.

She turned hoping to thank the stranger, but he had already descended the steps and was crossing the street. Frowning, she shook out her skirt and petticoat, starting off at a rather slower, more cautious pace to the mercantile.

"Oh, land o' mercy! Kat, what happened to you?" Mrs. Forester slapped her hand over her mouth as Kat stepped into the store. Taking in Kat's bedraggled appearance, the hand fell away, her facial muscles working hard to keep the smile from her face.

Kat gave her a thin-lipped response. "A little accident."

"You're a mess!" She crossed the room and took the package from Kat's hand. In a moment she had placed a comforting arm around her. "Mary Beth, watch the store for me."

Mrs. Forester and her husband lived in the back of the store in modest but cozy quarters. She ushered Kat to a chair by the wood stove. Pouring water from a pitcher into a bowl, she stepped aside to grab some towels from her bedroom.

Kat washed her hands and squinting into the mirror, she scrubbed away the smear on her face.

While she did, Mrs. Forester clucked sympathetically, brushing away the worst of the caked mud on her skirt hem. "What in the world, girl? It's like the days when you'd come in here, your nose bloody, or your knuckles bruised from fighting with Liam and his bunch of no-goods." She looked up at Kat's face. "Remember? You'd come in here looking like some poor alley cat, and I'd clean you up and plop you down, right there." She gestured to the stool by the wood stove. She squinted up into Kat's grinning face. "Seems I even put a stitch right there in that lower lip once."

Kat touched her lip, recalling the pain of it. "Pretty good nursing without training." She pursed her lips inspecting the tiny scar in the mirror. "There's barely a sign of it now."

The older woman stood with fists fastened to her hips. "You were quite the hellion back then, acting more like a badger than a squirt of a girl."

"And you'd scold me for not behaving like a lady, then you'd laugh and I knew you didn't much mind that I didn't."

Mrs. Forester shook her head, using the chair to pull herself to her feet. "You're right. Guess I was too much of a tomboy myself when I lived with my grandma back in Virginia. She spoiled me something awful." She laughed as she washed her hands before pouring two cups of tea from the pot simmering on the wood stove. Handing one to Kat, she then sat at the little cloth-covered table near the window. Patting the seat next to her, she said, "Now just you come and have a seat over here and tell me how the tomgirl turned into the lady."

Kat spent a pleasant morning sharing the trials and joys she'd experienced over the missing years since she'd left Snowberry as a very frightened but determined girl of sixteen. Telling Mrs. Forester of her hard journey to earning her degree was cathartic in a way. She told it as if narrating a story, almost dispassionately, describing the cruel pranks she'd endured at the hands of the young men who thought her unsuited for medicine. She could even laugh at them now as she stepped into the role of storyteller.

"Kat, I wouldn't have believed anyone else but you could have gotten through such humiliation and unjust treatment! You were always trying to make the bullies answer for what they did. I remember when you came in one day with a paper star pinned on your shirt. You'd gone and appointed yourself a lawman. Even now, it makes me laugh to think of your serious face, lower lip sticking out, hands on your hips, telling me how you weren't going to let that Liam pick on the little ones anymore." Mrs. Forester went to refill Kat's cup. She paused arrested at the window.

"Look at that, Kat! Remember when we could look out this window at the wide valley rolling out to the river? Now I'm looking at Mrs. Dugan's unmentionables hanging outside her back door." She seemed to step out of the present as Kat studied her face. "The town's changing too fast for me."

Kat's forehead wrinkled as she saw not one but a half-dozen more homes stretched out in a neat row where only grass and wildflowers had grown six years before.

"You said it was Ethan Hall who helped you out there?" Mrs. Forester pulled herself back to the moment when Kat saw her face brighten.

Kat lifted an eyebrow as she answered. "Yes, the same."

"Handsome, isn't he?" Mrs. Forester wasn't one to mince words.

"I suppose, if you like the Adonis type."

Mrs. Forester choked, laughing at Kat's response. Recovering, she leaned forward conspiratorially and patted Kat's arm. "He's a fine-looking young man. Even I can feel something stirring when I look into those blue eyes, if you know what I mean." She sat back and took another sip of tea. "He's quite the catch for a town like this."

Kat found herself stiffening, a flare of temper rising yet again. "I would hope that *should* I be looking for a suitor, I would look a little higher than someone who was ranked, just, better than worse." She caught the amusement in Mrs. Forester's eye and relaxed. "Besides, I'm not fishing."

"And why not, child? I mean seeing you come back here without a husband was quite a surprise. As pretty and smart as you are, well, there must have been many a fellow asking."

Kat idly turned her teacup on its saucer. "Well, you see I made a vow to myself. I knew it would take every bit of energy and grit to make it through school. If I allowed myself to be distracted by a romantic entanglement, I knew I'd never make it through."

"Well, you've certainly got grit! Anyone who knows you, knows that."

"But I needed self-discipline too." She sat back in her chair looking past Mrs. Forester out the window. "There were temptations, one in particular." The face of Caleb, the third-year student floated before her mind's eye. Her ear lobe throbbed at the memory.

"Well? Aren't you going to tell me?" Eyes bright with interest, her friend had leaned forward expectantly.

Kat waved her hand. "Not worth telling, really. But it taught me that I needed to be a little stricter with myself and employ some boundaries around my head and heart. So. . ." She leaned forward to whisper across the table. "I think of them as patients. And if a young man is *especially* attractive, I think of him as a cadaver."

Mrs. Forester's hand flew to her mouth. "Isn't that what they call a dead person?"

"Yes!" Kat laughed in a most unladylike fashion.

"Oh, and there's one other thing I do that reminds me to keep my focus on my career."

"Can't even imagine."

"When my mind starts to wander too far and I notice too much about. . .*things*, I pinch my ear. The harder I pinch, the better!"

Mrs. Forester wagged her head. "You are a caution, Kat! You plan on doing that all your life?"

"Not necessarily, but at least until I've worked a few years and have established a practice. Perhaps."

The door creaked, admitting a flushed, harried face. "Mrs. Forester, sorry to bother you, but I think you better talk to Mrs. Halverson about her order. She's kinda getting hot under the collar."

Mrs. Forester rolled her eyes and answered, "All right, Mary Beth. I'll be right there."

Kat remembered her reason for coming and picked up the soiled package from the floor. "Mrs. Forester, I forgot. Do you think you could alter a skirt that I have?"

"You do look a bit slimmer than I remember. You want me to take in the waist?"

Kat shook her head. "No, I was hoping you could make it into a split skirt, something that would make riding easier."

Mrs. Forester tipped her head, her interest piqued.

"It's a style I once saw in a magazine. I think there's plenty of fabric in this skirt."

"Leave it and I'll take a look. Sounds interesting. But you'll probably have to come back a few times and try it on for me." Mrs. Forester patted Kat's shoulder. "You can sit here awhile and I can make you some lunch in a bit. I won't be long."

Kat stood when she did. Noticing the dried pieces of mud about her, she said, "I'll just sweep up the mess I made and then be on my way. I wanted to do some more errands for Papa. Besides he's offered to buy lunch for me at the boarding house."

Mrs. Forester, her eyes soft with affection, said, "I sure have missed you, sweetheart."

Kat crossed the room and embraced her. "I've missed you, more than you know."

True to her word, Kat swept the floor clean of the dirt she'd brought with her. She'd even managed to shake loose most of the mud soiling her skirt hem, but she doubted the petticoat would ever be white again.

As she passed through the shop, she caught Mrs. Forester's eye and waved, mouthing a silent thank you. Mrs. Forester winked back at her.

Stepping out of the store, she squinted against the bright light of mid-day, lifting her hand to shield her eyes. She missed her bonnet, and thought that perhaps she could find something a little less stylish and more serviceable. *Well, when in Rome. . .*

Kat stepped to the edge of the walkway. Looking down, she scrutinizing the muddy road with no little concern. She looked left and right hoping to find a drier route across the street, but seeing none she took a tentative step down. *All right, I can do this.* Lifting her skirts two inches higher, she took another step. *Slow and steady.* With the next step she felt her boot slip into an unexpectedly deep puddle. Her ankle turned and her arms wind-milled in a last-ditch effort to stay upright.

The ground rose up, brown and wet. It was all dreadfully familiar. The next moment, a hand grabbed her elbow and another hand slipped around her waist. She said a silent prayer, not of gratitude. *Oh Lord, not him again!* Was he following her? She looked up into the face, not of Ethan Hall, but the stranger who'd tried to help her earlier.

"Steady there, Miss. Here, let me help you onto the walkway again." He held her securely by the hand. With his other hand firmly about her waist, he swung her effortlessly onto the step. Until she stood on her own with her hand securely gripping the railing, he kept his hand against her back to steady her.

Kat felt the awkward warmth in her cheeks and turned away, stepping onto the boardwalk. She wouldn't blush because of a mere touch, like a school girl! Lifting her chin, she forced herself to look directly into his eyes.

He was older than she'd first thought; the gray at his temples and slightly peppered hair might suggest he was into his late thirties. Anatomy class observations, strictly clinical curiosity, she told herself. He had a wiry frame topped by unusually wide shoulders. His face marked by a strong Roman nose, wide mouth and very nice lips that now parted into a smile. She cast her eyes down, finished with *clinical* curiosity. *What's wrong with me?*

He hesitated on the step. "Miss, um, where are you trying to go? Maybe I can help."

Kat composed herself, patting her hair back in place. "I'm supposed to meet my father at the boarding house down the street. Thank you, but I think I can manage. It's just a little mud."

He seemed to have arrived at a solution to her problem. "If you don't mind my offer, Adam and I have the wagon loaded and ready to head out. We could drive you there."

Kat looked at the wagon he indicated with his glance. It was but a few steps away, but she shook her head. "No, that's an imposition. Really, it isn't that far." She gazed at the pools of mud, a forlorn expression forcing the brave smile from her face.

"Really, it's no bother. Here!" He offered her his hand and called to the boy in the wagon. "Adam make room for the lady." Adam grinned down at her and scooted to the center of the bench seat. Jonathan guided her the few steps to the side of the wagon. Putting both hands around her waist, he lifted her to the wagon step. The boy, a wide grin on his face, helped pull her the rest of the way.

Forcing her skirt into the narrow space between the boy and the side of the wagon, Kat sat stiffly, her back pressed against the short back of the wagon seat. She glanced over at Adam and gave a tight-lipped smile. Feeling compelled to say something, she mumbled with a nervous laugh. "This is so much trouble."

Her rescuer swung up into the driver's side and took the reins from the boy. He kissed to the horses and the wagon started with a slurping sound as the wheels churned through the mire. To keep from falling, Kat grabbed the side of the seat. They traveled one block before Jonathan pulled the horses to the left and made a tight turn to head in the opposite direction. It took mere minutes to pull up directly in front of the boarding house. After handing the reins to Adam again, Jonathan hopped down with a splash, and passed behind the wagon, holding on as he did to keep from slipping. He lifted his hands to Kat.

Gathering her skirt in her hand, she balanced on the running board. He slid his hands around her waist for the second time and lifted her from the wagon to the sidewalk. He held her for only a heartbeat, but in that moment as he stood close to her, she noticed that his eyes were not brown as she had first thought but dark blue-gray. What a lovely shade of gray, she thought, and . . . *symmetrical!* They're *symmetrical*! Kat employed her well-rehearsed method of distraction. She recited it, like a catechism. *Step out of yourself, Kat! Don't be a silly fool. Keep your focus on your goal and don't get distracted. This is simple animal attraction!*

He released her and she took a step back.

"Thank you." She realized then that she did not know his name, nor had she introduced herself. She should at least be courteous.

Extending her hand to him, she said, "I'm sorry I didn't introduce myself before. I'm Kathryn Meriwether. . . *Dr.* Kathryn Meriwether."

"Jonathan Winthrop." He took her hand lightly, tipping his hat. "Nice to meet you, ma'am."

That was when she recognized the Texas drawl.

Carefully navigating his way through the mud at the back of the wagon, he stepped back into the wagon. When he saw that she hadn't moved from the step, Jonathan asked quite seriously, "Are you going to be all right?"

She wondered at this last comment, then realized she was still standing in the same place he'd left her, like a stunned deer in the crosshairs. "Oh, quite! Thank you." She lifted her hand to her ear lobe, pulling it viciously as she spun and stepped through the door of the boarding house.

Adam looked over at Jonathan, a sly smile creeping across his youthful face. "Good-lookin', huh?"

Jonathan looked at the boy with a bemused expression. "You interested, now? Don't you think she's a bit old for you?"

Adam colored. "Not too old to notice." He mumbled this, but shot back, "She's certainly not too old for you!"

Jonathan shrugged. "No, but I'm a bit too old for her, I reckon." He kissed to the horses and they leaned into their traces pulling the loaded wagon through the mud.

Adam settled down on the wagon seat. Half to himself he said, "She's sure a little thing, not much taller than me I guess."

Jonathan nodded once, commenting dryly, "Would guess that's true."

The boy stared off into the distance, his voice suddenly soft and dreamy. "But she's sure got all she needs tucked in between her pretty little head and those tiny feet."

Jonathan turned his head to study the boy. He shoved his fist hard into the boy's arm. "Adam! What kind of talk is that? Would your father want you talking about a lady like that?"

Adam flushed crimson. "Guess not." He stuck his chin out, shooting back. "But it's true."

Jonathan turned back to the road. "That it is. That it is."

For a moment he considered the fetching Dr. Meriwether, and had to agree with Adam's appreciation of her attractive qualities. Then he grinned at himself in wry amusement. He *was* a man nearly twice her age. Entertaining romantic notions might have been something he'd done before life had laid him low, but not now. What did he have to offer any woman? He was broken and he knew it, broken in a way no doctor could heal.

Chapter 6

Sheriffs Bullies and Liars

EIGHT OUT OF the original nine cans lay on the other side of the fence rail, pierced through. Kat lowered her rifle and squinted at the result of her firing. "Missed one!" She swore softly under her breath.

"Kat! When did you start swearing? You never heard that from me!" Nathaniel gave her a look of mock rebuke.

"Well, Papa, you pick up more than medical terms when you work with men under pressure." She threw back a rueful smile and reloaded.

Nathaniel nodded toward the execution line of soup and bean cans. "You seem to have lost a little of your irritating talent for beating me at target shooting. What's thrown your aim off?"

"Lack of practice, I suppose. Didn't have much time for it." She drew the weapon to her shoulder and fired. The final can flew up with a satisfying *plink*. "Too busy learning how to swear," Kat grinned at her father, handing him the Browning rifle, then picking up a half-dozen tin cans. She scrambled up the hill to balance them on the rail.

"Suppose none of those city doctors even know the business end of a gun from the butt," Nathaniel called after her as he leaned back against a tree trunk watching his daughter, skirt tucked into her waistband stride back down the hill and across the yard.

"Oh, they were quite familiar with back ends—just not those constructed of wood."

Nathaniel sniggered, "Kat! I'm afraid your feminine sensibilities have been compromised by your studies of anatomy."

"Papa, my feminine sensibilities were compromised long ago by being brought up by a doctor. Besides, it seems you were the one who raged at anyone who chose to use euphemisms instead of. . . Let's see. What did you say? Oh yes, 'perfectly adequate anatomical language.'"

Loading two .45 rounds, Kat pulled the Browning rifle back to her shoulder and fired, levering rapidly before taking a second shot. Two shots, two cans flying.

Nathaniel shook his head as he watched a sparkle of smug self-satisfaction brighten her eyes. "You know, for a while when you were growing up, I thought you just might decide to study law."

Kat picked up her father's gun, a newer Browning, and inspected it. "Now what in the world would have made you think that? You treated me like an intern most of my adolescence! Remember that I was the one who told Josie the real facts of life, thanks to you and a particularly well-illustrated medical book."

Nathaniel snorted. "I suppose I did. But you were darn good at picking up anything I taught you. You were doctoring everything from that ugly old yellow cat you carried around like a sack of potatoes, to wild rabbits. Couldn't have you sued for malpractice on the neighborhood pets!"

Kat spun to the target, the rifle loaded and fired.

"No, it was that you were always so keen on seeing that justice was served. Remember the Robinson children and that gang of Liam Brewster's?"

Kat bent down, picking up two spent rifle shells. She tumbled them in her hand while she thought back to her childhood vigilante days. She chuckled. "Guess, I did have a single-minded focus on delivering justice to those bullies."

Nathaniel sniffed at that. "Single-minded focus? You delivered it all right! They never went after those poor kids again after you *justiced* them bloody." Her father chuckled. "I tried to straighten that nose of his, but it ended up pointing two degrees south when he was facing due east."

"He still lives around here?" Kat squinted into the sun, taking a reading on the time.

"I see him from time to time. He's still a bully."

Kat cradled the barrel into the fold of her arm, starting off toward the house. Their talk of her vigilante days brought the self-appointed sheriff to mind. That started her mind traveling down another path. Hadn't most of the gold and silver strikes been outside the ranges bordering their long valley?

"Papa, why are the ore wagons even coming on this side of the mountain and not using the old road?"

"Well, they were for a time, I think. From what I've heard, the route held too many places for robbers to ambush the wagons. Our side of the mountain makes the trip through more open land. It's safer. Or, at first it was. Now, I hear they take a different route from time to time, trying to confuse the robbers."

Kat kicked at a clod of mud. "Men and their fool lust for quick riches! How many lives and towns been ruined by it?"

"I assume that's a rhetorical question," Nathaniel said.

"It's going to change the town! It already has! There'll be more drinking establishments, more gambling, and more violence." Her eyes flashed with anger as she imagined what she feared would become the town's inevitable future.

"You're preachin' to the choir, Kat. Don't you think I've already seen the results in my office here? I never used to treat gunshot wounds, unless you count the time Mrs. McDougal moved her husband's rifle to dust the mantle and accidentally shot him in the foot."

"She was the only one claiming it was an accident, as I recall," Kat skipped up the steps and onto the porch that wrapped around the house from the kitchen entry to the office front door. "Mr. McDougal was singing quite a different song in your surgery." Nathaniel chuckled and bobbed his head at the memory, taking her gun from her and carrying both inside the house. Kat sat on the porch bench where she had an expansive view of the town below and the river beyond, meandering away down the long valley.

She was glad that her father and mother had agreed to build the house on the hill rather than in the heart of town. Some people complained about having to make the climb, especially those with rheumatism, but Nathaniel was never one to deny a request for a house call. So, it became a non-issue.

Up here away from the center of town, the child she'd been felt free of critical eyes, especially so after her mother's death. Her father had indulged her to be...different, a little wild by others' more conventional standards. More than one opinionated, *concerned* citizen had admonished her father to use a tighter hand in raising her. But Doc Meriwether had ignored them, just like he'd ignored his sister's advice to send her back east to her so she could be raised in a *civilized* town and taught how to be a proper lady. And there'd been those that tried to arrange a wife and mother to fill the needs of the widower and child. Nathaniel was, after all, quite a catch and still an attractive man. But he'd successfully escaped those efforts, remaining a contented bachelor.

Kat reached up, pulling the pins from her hair. Her long plait of brown hair swung down over her shoulder. Leaning her head against the house wall, she closed her eyes. The winds, brisk but not cold, felt pleasant brushing over her bare arms. The smell of spring filled the air better than any perfume, and soon the scent of her mother's blush roses would add to the heady fragrance. Even before that, the lilac bushes bordering the small garden would paint a lavender backdrop for the sweet peas that would follow with tender shoots of pink and purple reaching up and up.

Opening her eyes again, she felt a shadow of melancholy steal some of the day's warmth, realizing that she might not still be here to see them bloom. Her hand slipped into the pocket of her skirt, and pulling out the letter from St. Mary's Hospital, she read it once more.

"What you got there? You sure you don't have some beau back east who's writing you love poems?" Nathaniel had slipped quietly from the house onto the porch without her hearing him.

Hastily folding the letter, she slipped it back into her pocket. "No!" She took his hand and pulled him down to the bench beside her. Threading her arm through his, she lay her head on his shoulder, breathing in the familiar scent of him, a peculiar mixture of camphor and chamomile soap. "You know I've got room in my life for only one man and the position is filled."

Nathaniel looked down at her, his voice soft and colored with a tint of sadness. "That's what worries me, Kat. Can you really be happy here? You had so much to keep you there, young doctors and new medicine must have enticed you to stay. And here you are with this old frontier doctor."

Maybe this was her opportunity. Maybe she could show him the letter, then tell him how exciting it would be to be a part of a new hospital in a bustling town like San Francisco. He'd understand the opportunity it opened for her. She reached into her pocket.

Her father spoke before she could. "Kat, I had something made for you. I've had it since before you came home, but wasn't sure if you were ready for it. Maybe you aren't, but..." He gave her a nervous smile. In lieu of explanation, he pulled a neatly wrapped parcel from the side of the bench and onto his lap, something he'd apparently carried onto the porch without her knowledge.

Curiosity stirred and she took the package onto her own lap. She looked up at him, eyes questioning.

"Go ahead. Open it!" His face became a peculiar mixture of boyish joy and apprehension.

Kat tore open the edge, pulling the paper away to reveal a plank of wood with metal hooks at the top. Seeing it unwrapped left her more baffled. She looked up at him again, puzzled.

"Turn it over, silly!"

She obeyed.

It was a neatly inscribed sign that read:

Dr. Kathryn Meriwether

&

Dr. Nathaniel Meriwether

Kat ran her finger over the crisp blue lettering, lingering over the title before her name. Her chest suddenly tight, she feared looking her father in the face.

"Papa...it's beautiful!" She turned to him, throwing her arms around his neck, managing not to look into his eyes or for him to see into her own. "Thank you," she whispered into his whiskered cheek.

His voice, husky with emotion, answered her, "You're welcome, little girl." He kissed her cheek. "I'm so proud of you."

Tears dripping onto his coat, she clung to him. "You are a dear. I love you, Papa." Kat pulled away, dragging her sleeve across her eyes. "Look at me! I'm such a baby!"

Still unwilling to look at him directly, she scooped up the sign and wrapping paper, then turned away, her heels rapidly beating a retreat across the porch. "I'll make us some lunch, all right?" she called over her shoulder.

Nathaniel remained on the bench, his eyes following her as she swept across the porch and into the kitchen. It wasn't the reaction he'd imagined. Before he had the time to ask her anything, the sound of a wagon being driven up the hill at a rapid rate drew his attention to the road. Hearing the shout of the driver, Kat stepped back onto the porch.

"Doc, we found the guard!" The man shouting at her father was not someone Kat recognized. He looked haggard and nearly frantic.

"He's been shot up pretty bad!" he called from the driver's seat.

As they pulled into the yard, Kat saw that one other man sat in the back with the injured man. Before the wagon had come to a stop, the man riding in back jumped down. While all three men carried the guard into the examining room, Kat led the horses the rest of the way up to the house.

When Kat stepped into the office, she pulled an apron from the wall hook and stepped up to the examining table across from her father. The patient's face was ashen, his breathing coming in rasping gasps.

"We've been searching for the last two days. I heard him groan when I passed the place we'd searched yesterday near Bear Rock. I couldn't believe he was still alive."

Nathaniel looked up at Kat and made a slight nod of his head to the man's chest. Now that his clothing had been cut away, Kat could see the wound that had opened the man's chest. Shotgun, she thought, and close range. The man was drowning in his own blood.

The man coughed, blood spilling from his mouth, scarlet on white lips. Kat heard him trying to form words, gasps really. She leaned closer to his face turning her ear close to his lips.

He said the word twice more, then gave another strangled cough. Then there was silence, punctuated only by his last death rattle. His eyes no longer squeezed shut in pain, he lay with them open, staring into eternity.

"Did you hear what he said? Did it make sense? I heard him trying to talk earlier, but couldn't make it out."

Kat straightened and turned to the men. "I think he said 'law' or it could have been 'lawman.'"

The driver stared down at the guard. "Maybe he wanted us to tell the law. Poor devil. This was his first run."

Kat doubted the man's conjecture, but what else could the guard have been wanting them to know? But there was something far more disturbing about her examination of the man's injuries, and by the look on her father's face she deduced that he too had made the same observation. For some reason he seemed to keep it to himself and so she did not voice her own concerns. But she was certain that this gunshot wound was *not* two days old. No one would have lasted so long with that amount of blood loss and type of injury. He'd been shot within hours of them finding him, not days. That was something a first-year student would have known.

The men carried the guard's body back to the wagon. They'd take him to the livery where a coffin would be constructed. He'd be buried by tomorrow afternoon, along with any evidence his body might provide for further investigation.

Kat stood beside her father on the porch watching the wagon slowly move off down the road, the guard's body wrapped in a sheet, now stained red. For long moments she waited for her father to speak of what they'd both observed. When he walked into the house without saying a word, she followed.

"Papa, why didn't you tell them the man had to have been shot *today*, last night at the earliest?"

Nathaniel Meriwether sat heavily in a chair at the kitchen table, and pulled a hand slowly across his face. He looked older in the dim lantern light, shadows hollowing his eyes and mouth. Kat could hold her tongue no longer. "Papa, why didn't you tell them?"

"Honey, it's complicated." Her father bowed over the table, palms pressed together, thumbs pressed to his forehead. A casual onlooker might mistake the posture for either prayer or the misery of a drunkard.

Kat sat opposite him waiting, knowing that in time he would explain. He always did. Even when she was just a child, he'd take the time to explain things she would understand only in the years to come. But his openness with her had helped to form a special bond of trust.

"Something's going on that just doesn't add up. There's been the sudden change in route for the wagons carrying ore from the mines, the growing number of men who seem to have money to spend in town, but no livelihood, and then there's the sheriff's vigilantes. Even with the increase in *lawmen*," he said it like he meant to say 'miscreants,' "the violence hasn't decreased. The simple explanation is that I don't know who to trust anymore."

Shadows deepened the creases of his brow. She studied him with the eye of a daughter, rather than a physician. At his age, he should be creating laugh lines around his eyes, the memory of smiles at the corners of his lips. Every new line that marked his face was graven by fear and worry. His joy and relief at her return was cast in a new light as she realized the strain he had been enduring alone. Night time emergency calls, mutterings in the town, his own dark premonitions - all evidence that very soon, one doctor would not be enough to serve the needs of this town.

Kat rose and circumnavigated the tiny table. From behind, she wrapped her arms around his chest and pressed her cheek against the top of his head, enfolding all of him - his worries and cares - in the comfort of her presence. "Then we'll just have to trust each other."

Paper crinkled against her thigh. In her pocket, her secret sat heavy as an ingot of silver.

Shifting Perspectives

WITH TENDRILS OF steam puffing from its nostrils into the morning air, the calf pulled itself awkwardly onto shaky legs to stand weaving for long moments before collapsing in a heap to the ground again. He stretched his neck and bellowed to his mother who stood but a few yards away, munching on frost-crisp shoots of grass. Turning her head, she answered with a louder more resonant *moo*. Once more, the calf hoisted itself in one great lunge to its feet.

Jonathan slouched comfortably in the saddle, his heavy coat buttoned to his throat to keep out the last attempts of winter to hold onto its claim of the high valley. Silently watching the mother and calf, Adam stood nearby holding the reins of his horse.

He whispered to Jonathan, "Can I touch him? The calf, can I touch him?"

Jonathan straightened as his mare shifted her weight from one leg to the other. Studying the cow before giving the boy an answer, he threw the boy a half-cocked smile and nodded. "Take it easy, so as not to bother his mother. She might take exception even to a pup like you."

Adam handed his reins to Jonathan and stalked warily across the new spring grass. This was not yet the lush valley it would become in late spring when the sun would shine down benevolently upon the meadows and low foothills, bringing warmth and new growth. His footfalls made soft squelching sounds in the moist earth still saturated by melting snow. Adam stopped when he was ten feet from the calf, the two eyeing each other with curiosity.

With infinitesimal movements, Adam reached out his hand to the calf. Its tongue extended, stretching toward the boy's fingers with curiosity. Adam took another cautious step forward, slipping a bit on the wet grass. The calf took a shaky step back and gave a low *moo*. The boy tried again, a step forward and fingers again inviting the calf forward. With its soft wet tongue, the calf met the boy's fingers.

Adam's face cracked wide open with a smile of delight. "He sucked on my finger," he whispered, ecstatic and reverential all at once. Like he'd just had his first kiss, rather than been sampled for edibility by a calf.

Something about the moment drew out of Jonathan a distant, deeply half-hidden memory, one from when he was a boy even younger than Adam. That look of wonder on Adam's face, the slightly open mouth, body inclined toward this new living thing called up a memory, long buried. For

Jonathan, it had been a colt lying next to its mother in their barn. The smell of wet straw, manure, horse sweat, and blood encased the moment forever in the boy's memory. He'd been drawn to that new life just as Adam was to the calf, drawn to the wonder of it.

When was the last time he'd experienced the wonder of anything? But here it was, a surprise as beautiful as the fresh smell of morning in the mountains.

Adam slowly moved his hand, reaching for the calf's delicate muzzle. Ever so gently, he stroked it. Jonathan observed the slight lowering of tense shoulders in both the boy and calf at that moment of contact. A fleeting moment of trust held them there. Jonathan found himself pulled into the magic of it. Years of harsh reality that had left him jaded, blinded to the simple pleasures were, for a brief time, forgotten.

Jonathan pulled his gaze from the scene to the rich pasture land that stretched a mile on either side of the river. A man could make a good home for himself in such a place as this, where grass grew plentifully and the river flowed down from high mountain springs through every season. In his mind's eye he saw a modest cabin nestled on the low rise at the far side of the valley where it would command a view of two mountain ranges, with rugged peaks snow-capped in winter and verdant green in summer.

"How old do you think he is?" Adam asked softly.

Jonathan returned his attention to the boy, not answering right away. "Looks to me, he's not more than a few hours old."

"He's a beauty, isn't he?"

Jonathan checked himself from responding with a wry remark. Seeing the boy's enraptured expression, he looked once more and saw the calf as the boy did. The perfectly formed ears, the wide nose that would function just as it should, the sturdy legs designed to carry him for miles across rocky terrain or muddy grasslands, his short brown hair, a perfect match to his mother's sleek coat, made him beautiful indeed. So, Jonathan simply nodded to the boy's question that was not a question.

But Jonathan also noted the bloodied earth where the cow's after-birth had stained it crimson. Something beautiful had come from pain. As suddenly as the moment had transported him to a state of pleasurable memories, he fell back into the vision that held him captive for these many months. Again, he was there staring down at the snow, stained red by the girl's blood. He shivered and closed his eyes tight, forcing the memory back down into the dark place that bound it. There it remained protected by a door that, against his will, swung both ways.

"What were you thinking!" Ethan, face burning with a combined fuel of frustration and anger, raged at the man who slouched sullenly against the wall.

Liam Brewster's reply powered across the room, thrown at Ethan like a rock in a school yard fight. "I did what needed being done! He pulled a gun on me! And he'd have talked as sure as anything if I hadn't killed him!"

Ethan chewed on the corner of his lip, his hands hanging stiff at his sides, clenching and unclenching. He shook his head in disgust, then turned from Liam to Noah, a stoop-shouldered giant, with downcast eyes. "And you? What have you got to say for yourself? You were supposed to keep this one under control."

"I don't need no nursemaid!" Liam shot back.

"Oh, I think this proves you do," Ethan said without turning.

"He *did* try to talk us into taking out a part of the silver," Noah offered.

"There are ways to *deal* with problems that don't end with a dead body," Ethan growled. "Bodies leave trails, *gentlemen*.'" He strode three steps to the window, staring out across the open space to the paddocks beyond. He shook his head and spun back to face them. "And you left one obvious trail. You could have at least disposed of it somewhere else and they might have believed he simply made off with the shipment. Did either of you think of that!"

"It just didn't seem right to leave him there. I thought his family might...you know." Noah stuttered to a halt when he saw Ethan's face.

Ethan blew in disgust. "But it was all right to shoot him." He shook his head slowly, chewing on his lower lip, then spoke his thoughts aloud. "Well, if the men who found him don't figure out that he wasn't shot where they found him, Doc Meriwether and his daughter are sure to. That will raise questions."

Ethan spun back to the window. The attractive face of Kat Meriwether materialized in Ethan's mind's eye. He had no desire to think of her as the enemy. In fact, under different circumstances, he might even convince her to yield a bit of that educated aloofness to see him in a favorable light.

More and more he felt ensnared, like a rabbit, not like the clever man he prided himself to be, one who could always out think his enemy. He knew how to use his wits to avoid using force. These brutes had no such mental acuity. But one thing was certain. He was *not* going to hang for murder. That was unthinkable.

More to himself than to the two men he muttered, "And somehow, I have to fix this."

Chapter 8

Lost Places of Solitude

JOSIE SWUNG HER legs over the side of the bed as Kat stepped to the basin to wash her hands. "I don't think you'll make it to the end of the month for this one to be born."

Patting her swollen belly, Josie laughed. "My babies have always been impatient. They all seem in a hurry. Still are."

Kat dried her hands and closed her medical bag before taking a seat at the long kitchen table where the oldest girl of Josie's three children sat tearing strips of cloth. "What are you making Caroline?"

"Mama's teaching me how to sew a rag rug." The face that beamed up at Kat was just a younger version of her mother. This was the face of the girl she'd grown up with, her partner in mischief.

Kat knew the girl could be no older than six, but being the oldest, she was growing up quickly. Her mother would need her help even more with this new child. "Those are nice colors. My mama taught me to do that when I was a little girl, but not as little as you. You must be a great help to your mama."

"Oh, she is!" Josie declared. She carried two mugs of tea to the table and placed one in front of Kat before sitting across from her. She groaned softly as she eased herself to the chair. "Caroline, why don't you go on outside and play with those new kittens for a while. I know you've been dying to."

"Thank you, Mama." Caroline finished rolling the last strip of cloth she'd torn from her father's worn shirt. Before running out the door she turned to Kat. "Miss Kat, won't you come and see the kittens too?" She giggled and put her hand to her mouth. "That sounds funny. Miss Kat do you want to see the cats?" She giggled again.

Kat smiled. "Yes, it does. I'd love to see them. I'll do that before I go."

Caroline had barely closed the door when Josie leaned forward, eyes glowing with anticipation. "Now, Kat, tell me everything! You must have visited museums and restaurants and been adored by dozens of men. It must have been so exciting and romantic!"

Kat laughed lightly. "I tell you honestly, I spent most of my time with my nose in a book, studying until my eyes burned. It wasn't glamorous. And the only exciting part was the fearful kind that filled me with dread before every examination!"

Josie sat back, her hand pressing the small of her back. "Well, it had to be a lot more exciting than living here in Snowberry for the past four years."

"What I remember most was the hard work." Kat ran her fingers lightly over the table-cloth, recalling the long nights alone in her room with nothing more for company than the medical tomes piled about her desk.

Josie shook her head, disbelieving. "But your aunt? Didn't she introduce you to society? You certainly don't look much like the girl that left here! Look at you!" She waved at Kat as if her attire was evidence of the glamorous life she'd left behind.

Kat glanced down at her newly altered, split skirt. "This?" She laughed. "I asked Mrs. Forester to alter a skirt for me so I could ride more easily."

But she knew that wasn't all Josie was seeing. She *was* different. From her aunt, she'd learned how to carry herself with poise, how to dress to show off her best features, how to choose colors to flatter her complexion and hair. Even the leather jacket she wore now had been carefully tailored to flatter her figure, just shy of the skirt waistband to show off her slim waist. Delicate embroidery on the collar and cuffs softened the overall look.

"I always envied your thick hair, even when you wore it in braids. Now, you wear it up, so stylish!" Josie tipped her head, tucking a stray lock of her own pale hair behind an ear. She scowled. "But I still think you aren't being honest with me about the men you were with every day. Surely, one would have taken an interest in you!"

Kat examined her chewed thumbnail, before folding her hands in her lap. "There might have been one. But most of the male students resented me for being there, and the women only saw me as a threat, competition. So, on those rare occasions when I did go out, it was usually with my aunt to teas and ladies' social events."

"But there was one, wasn't there? I can tell. Remember? I'm your closest friend."

Kat rose to her feet and brought the kettle back to the table to fill their cups. "If you insist on knowing..."

Josie leaned forward. "Yes! I insist! He was handsome, wasn't he? Was he a doctor too?"

Blowing into her cup, Kat smiled at her friend's obvious hunger for a romantic tale. She knew she'd be disappointed at the truth.

"There was a third-year student that was one of the few men who treated my interest in medicine seriously. But the other one was a rather good-looking man I met through my aunt's friend. He was British. He wasn't a doctor, and that's probably why we saw each other more than once." Kat sat down again, and looked up at her friend's eager face, amused. She couldn't help herself. The moment invited her to take advantage of her friend's gullibility.

"Well, it was sad, really," Kat began dramatically. "We seemed to be getting along so well. He took me to dinner three weekends in a row. We even attended the opera, *The Marriage of Figaro*. It was quite lovely. The costumes were elegant, brocades and velvets, and more lace than you could ever imagine."

Josie's eyes widened. Her hand fluttered to her throat. "Did you wear white? I've heard that it's very fashionable. Did you wear long white gloves?"

Kat nodded. "And my aunt loaned me her mother's pearl necklace."

Josie clapped her hands gleefully. "I can just see you! Oh, how heads must have turned when you walked in."

"I think I was just one amidst many young women and jewel bedazzled ladies of society."

"And I think you're just too modest, Kat Meriwether! You had the boys here crazy when you were wearing your papa's pants. I can only imagine what they thought when they saw you dressed up."

Kat laughed at that. Then she lifted her hand and rested it lightly on her cheek, affecting a tragic countenance for her audience of one. "But sadly, I learned that night that. . ." She paused for effect, embellishing the drama by touching her finger to the corner of her eye as if to wipe away a tear.

Josie leaned further forward, holding her breath.

"I learned that night that he was an embezzler. He'd made a fortune abroad, working at the Bank of England. He was on the run from the police, and there was a bounty on his head." Kat glanced up at her friend's face, and knew she had hooked her right through the lip. But that wasn't enough for Kat. She wanted to pull her fully on shore and watch her flop there.

She lowered her voice to a whisper. "And he was wanted *dead* or alive!"

Josie gasped, sitting back so suddenly that she spilled her tea. "Oh no!" Her hand flew to her gaping mouth. "Dead or alive?"

"I had no choice. I had to discourage any further relationship. I knew that I could never marry a thief." Kat shook her head sadly, but the mischief playing at the corner of her mouth betrayed her.

"Kat! You little devil! You made that up!" Josie huffed with disgust.

Kat leaned forward, her elbows on the table, her cup in her hands and casually asked, "You wanted a story, didn't you?"

They laughed together until Josie started to hiccup. Kat poured a cup of water for her to drink, still laughing.

After she'd regained control of her diaphragm, Josie asked, "Was any part of the story true?"

Kat's mouth curved upward and she shrugged. "Some of it. He was British, and handsome, and he did take me to the opera. I did like him, quite a lot. But I did not reject him. He rejected me."

Josie looked at her, mouth slightly open, eyes full of questions.

"When he knew that I was serious about my medical studies, and that I was unwilling to give them up for anything or any*one*, he wished me well, and simply said goodbye. It was rather . . .an abrupt ending."

"Oh, Kat!" Josie's hand flew to her mouth again.

Kat waved her hand as if waving away the memory like an annoying fly. "I'm quite over him. You don't have to feel sorry for me. Life is filled with choices. For the most part, I'm satisfied with mine."

Josie lifted an eyebrow. "Really?"

"Really!"

"I can't imagine what that must be like. To have choices, I mean. Getting married to the first man who asked me. Having babies every year since."

"But you seem happy." Kat wanted it to be true for her friend.

Josie laughed again, genuine mirth this time. "I am. Truly, I am. I love my Simon. He's a good man and a wonderful father. But, you know, it might have been nice to have a choice. Feel like it all just happened, like life just comes with each new day like the sun and the seasons, one right after the other. Don't really have time to think about doing anything different, really. Even when it comes to what we eat, I make what's in the garden or what's been slaughtered." She smoothed the tablecloth with her fingers wide, but her unlined face reflected no sadness. She seemed to simply be making an honest assessment of her life, as if taking inventory.

Kat reached across the table and took her friend's hand. "Choices can be hard too. Choices can bring regrets as well."

Josie squeezed her hand. "Suppose so."

Josie insisted that Kat stay for lunch and so she did. They filled the morning with much embellished stories of their mischievous days and less-than-ladylike antics.

Kat washed up the dishes after lunch while Josie sat with her feet propped on a chair, doctor's orders. Soon after she gathered her things and Josie followed her out to where her mare was tied to the railing.

"I sure like the Morgan." Josie stroked the neck of the little mare. "She's sure pretty. What'd you decide to call her?"

"Blue. I know it's a bit silly, but I think it suits her." After tying on her medical bag, Kat patted her mare's rump. "Dad always knew how much I admired Mr. Forester's pair of morgans. He talked Mr. Forrester into letting him buy the filly the mare threw last spring."

Blue cocked her ears to Kat's voice and tossed her head, as if knowing she was the topic of discussion. Her blue gray coat made her unique among her breed and particularly attractive. Her petite stature made her perfectly suited to Kat's small frame.

"She's a beauty, isn't she? I think we might become the best of friends. She's a bit of a scamp."

"Like you!" Josie hugged her as best she could with her round belly. They laughed at that and Kat swung up into the saddle. The Morgan pranced to the side as she took up the reins.

"I'll be back as soon as you send word," Kat promised.

With a gentle nudge of her knees, the Morgan leaped forward. Kat reined her into a trot and started off down the trail back to town.

With the sun on her back and the Morgan anxious for a run, she made a decision to change direction. One place more than any other in all of Snowberry had called her home. She realized how much she needed to see it again. At the fork in the road she turned Blue's head to the trail leading into the little valley bordered by foothills.

As the path widened, she gave Blue her head. The trees grew closer together at the higher elevation, the air more fragrant. Kat leaned into the run, thrilling at the speed and the joy she sensed in the Morgan as she flew down the trail. This little mare was most happy running full out, and seemed to do it effortlessly.

The path led down to a low bank across a stream, then followed the base of the foothills before spilling out into the valley floor. Kat pulled up to a slow walk before leaving the tree line.

The narrow valley opened before her familiar and inviting, her private sanctuary. This was the place that she'd fled to when her mother had died. She'd found healing here, surrounded by the beauty of the mountains, the meandering stream, marshy edges of the meadow, and gentle foothills. She'd named it Lost Eden. No one else referred to it that way. It was known to the town's folk as Schmidt's Valley, named after the man who'd first claimed it and built a cabin for himself near the west side. She raised a hand to shield her eyes from the afternoon sun, straining to see if the little cabin was still standing. The last time she'd seen it, it appeared to be ready to collapse on itself.

On the low bench above the river she could make out the roof and chimney. Odd, she thought, there appeared to be fencing behind the house and another structure that had not been there before. She spoke to the blue roan, and she stepped up into a trot. Farther from the tree line she began to make out the rounded backs of grazing cattle scattered about the valley. At that same moment, she heard a voice call out to someone, and an answer returned. *They must be up the hill, out of sight in the trees, collecting strays perhaps.*

For some reason, she could not explain even to herself, she didn't want to be seen. Turning Blue's head, she kneed her into a run back the way they'd come, only pulling her up when they were within the cover of trees again. At that point, she turned in the saddle and looked back. Two men emerged from the trees several yards from where she'd heard their voices. Four steers preceded them into the valley as the men herded them back toward the homestead.

Things *had* changed. Her secret place of solitude was no longer hers alone. She turned and urged the mare back down the trail, a sense of loss enveloping her as she moved deeper into the sunless woods.

Chapter 9

Deferred Decisions

PAPA? WHO BOUGHT the old homestead in Schmidt's Valley?" Kat set the table while her father ladled stew into their bowls.

"Hmm. Let's see. I think I did hear that someone moved in up there last fall. Think it was a father and son," Nathaniel said as he carried two bowls to the table. "Why do you ask?" He licked his finger.

Kat shrugged. "I was up there yesterday after visiting with Josie. I could see that some work had been done on the place. Looks like he's running cattle in the valley." Taking a seat, she leaned over to take a sniff of the steaming stew.

"Nice place for it, year-round water, good grassland, pretty too." Nathaniel took a biscuit from a platter and handed it to his daughter.

Kat ate in silence. Nathaniel studying her face, noted the change in her countenance. It wasn't like Kat not to have something to flavor the conversation.

"I'm not sure I like the idea of you going up there on your own. This isn't the quiet place you left. We still don't know who's behind these robberies or where they're holed up. Could be anyone. Gold and silver seem to bring out the worst in folks." Nathaniel dipped his biscuit into the stew and contemplated it before saying anything more.

He changed the subject. "So how does Josie look? I warned her that she needed to be prepared to catch this one herself since she seems to deliver each baby quicker than the last." He chuckled.

Kat realized her father had asked her a question, and she hadn't heard it. "I'm sorry, Papa. What did you ask?"

Nathaniel shook his head and sat back in his chair. "How was the mare? Is she too much to handle? Since you haven't been riding for some time, I was concerned she might be needing a bit more training before you start to take her out on rounds."

Kat lifted her napkin to her mouth, a smirk peeking out of the corner. "Do you really think I'd turn down the challenge of a horse that was too fast?"

Nathaniel chuckled at that. "No. My little girl never backed down from any challenge, not those presented on four legs nor two."

With the letter firmly in her grip, Kat stepped determinedly into the post office. It had taken her hours to compose, and half a day more to decide to post it. She'd resolved to take the hospital position but had asked that they give her another month to settle her affairs at home. She did not elaborate on what those affairs might be. Knowing they had a real need, she felt quite certain they would grant her the extra time.

And she found it easy to justify the delay. Procrastination was something she'd a talent for. Her study habits had proved that, finding her mind worked better when the pressure was greatest. It was an odd quirk and she recognized it and used it to her advantage. She hoped that in that time, she might find a way to gently break the news to her father.

"Kat!" The postmaster who greeted her was also the owner of the general store, Mr. Forester. His office was adjacent to the store, a recent addition, not much larger than a generous privy. He liked the formality of a separate office for, as he called it, government business. He'd even had his wife sew him an American flag to hang at the door.

"Mr. Forester, nice to see you." Kat stepped into the room, and moved to the side, holding her skirt to make room to close the door. Less than five feet from the door was the counter.

Mr. Forester struck his forehead with the palm of his hand. "Sorry, I forgot! It's *Dr.* Kat now."

"I think I'd feel a little odd if you called me that, Mr. Forester. You've been a family friend far too long. Kat is just fine."

"Well then, what can the U.S. government do for you, Kat?" He leaned forward, his large hands spread wide on the counter.

"I need to post a letter to San Francisco."

He seemed impressed. "San Francisco is it?" Well, let's see. He pulled out a tattered book from beneath the counter.

"Well, that'll be a 10-cent Thomas Jefferson. That's the new brown one, you know. That shouldn't take much longer than a couple of weeks. The bag goes up to the VanWyck Station this afternoon. Good thing you brought it in today!"

"Kat! I thought that was your voice." Mrs. Forester squeezed through the door connecting the store and post office, forcing Mr. Forester into the corner where he stood wedged between two piles of boxes.

Kat felt more than a little uncomfortable in such close quarters. She'd have happily joined Mrs. Forester in the store if she'd asked.

"I wanted to ask you if you might lend a hand organizing the church picnic. It's a fund-raiser for the missionary society, you know. All for a good cause. I was telling the ladies that you must have all kinds of ideas you learned back east."

"Oh, I don't know about that." To Kat's way of thinking, organizing social gatherings seemed about as unpleasant a task as dissecting a bloated cadaver. No, that was at least interesting! "I'm sure you know far better what the town people would like."

Mrs. Forester took another step into the office, forcing her husband to grab the edge of the counter to keep from falling backward into the pile of boxes. "Nonsense! We need your help. Mrs. Townsend, Mrs. Schuster and I are meeting tomorrow afternoon right here. Now, I look forward to your ideas." Without waiting for a response, Mrs. Forester squeezed out of the room.

Kat, looking stunned, gave Mr. Forester a pained expression.

"Oh, Kat, there's nothing much you can do about it. I can tell you that from experience. When Mrs. Forester decides a thing, there ain't no way undeciding it."

Kat left the post office befuddled and not a little out of sorts. She seemed to be losing the tight control she'd held on her life up until returning to Snowberry. Two steps into the street and she realized she still held the letter in her hand.

"Oh bother!" Turning on her heel, she nearly collided with Ethan Hall.

"Excuse me," Kat said in a tone laced with irritation.

Smiling, Ethan tipped his hat. "No, Dr. Meriwether, excuse me."

Kat stepped to the side, eager to be on her way, away to where she might regain a little sense of her old self-confidence.

"Dr. Meriwether, I've been meaning to come see you and your father." Ethan's previous smile, replaced now with a solemn expression.

Kat hesitated. "Oh? Do you have a medical need?" She doubted it, but she knew that professional demeanor makes a great defense.

"Oh no! It's on official business, in my capacity as a lawman."

"I see." She waited, managing to keep her expression flat.

"It's part of my job to investigate all the circumstances of these recent robberies. I understand that you and your father may have information concerning the unfortunate death of the guard found recently."

She had an odd thought that the man was more attractive serious than when he was attempting to be charming. "Well, I'm not sure there's any more that we can tell you than the two men who found him have already probably stated. But I'm sure that my father would be happy to share any information that he has if you would care to speak with him." She was not about to tell him her own observations. "Now if you'll excuse me, I have a patient to see." Leaving him open mouthed, she walked away.

By the time she realized that the letter to the hospital was *still* in her hand, she was half-way up the hill to home. With a frown, she folded it and placed it in her pocket beside the hospital's offer of employment. She assured herself that she could mail it later.

Buried Secrets

KAT CUT THROUGH the tough stem and threw it behind her onto a growing pile of fruit tree suckers. She sat back on her heels and looked up at the crabapple tree already arrayed with magenta buds ready to burst open. The tree looked like it could breathe again. She rose to her feet and stepped back brushing dirt from the knees of her pants as she did.

"Much better! What do you think, Mama?" she said aloud. She hoped her mother would have been pleased to see that her hedge of crabapple trees, once so lovingly tended, was still thriving.

On either side of the trees, red peony stalks poked from the damp leaf-covered ground with a promise of pink and peach blooms yet to come. She lifted her dirt covered hands to her face and breathed in the pungent fragrance of moist, awakening soil, and closed her eyes with pleasure.

A voice, deep and sonorous, called across the yard. "Dr. Meriwether?"

She stepped from behind the row of trees and saw the man standing at the corner of the house. He seemed hesitant to walk farther into the garden, and waited for her to cross to him.

Kat recognized him as she drew closer. It was the man who'd gone to the trouble of driving her the few yards to the boarding house.

Jonathan tipped his hat as she approached him. "Dr. Meriwether, I was hoping to find your father home."

She brushed her hair from her face with a dirty hand. "He's not here at the moment. He had some house calls to make this afternoon. May I be of service?"

He shifted his weight and brought a hand to the back of his neck. "Well, it's my friend, you see. He needs a bit of doctoring."

Kat started for the office. "Oh, is he in the office now? I can help him."

"No. He's still at the cabin. He couldn't ride here, because of the injury, you see."

Kat turned back, waiting. He dropped his gaze to the dirt, apparently unwillingly to elaborate.

"Well then, let me get my bag and we'll ride there." She started for the door again. "I'll just be a minute."

"Are you sure your father won't be home soon?"

There it was again. She swung on him, ready to defend herself, but stopped when she saw his face. The look of discomfort made it clear to her that he was embarrassed, but why?

"What is the nature of his injury? Can we afford to wait for my father to return?" She had regained her composure and the question came levelly.

Jonathan blew out a breath of resignation. "He got into an argument with a mule."

Kat waited, resisting the urge to smile.

He pulled his hand across his face, and then seemed to have come to a decision. "The mule bit him."

"I think I can handle such an injury, even if he requires stitches."

Jonathan rubbed his chin. "You see, I think he'd be awful embarrassed if a woman treated him. It isn't...it's a problem of where he was bit."

Kat arched an eyebrow, even though she'd only wanted to maintain an expressionless professional demeanor. "So where is the bite?"

He cast his eyes to his boots and mumbled, "The mule got him in the caboose." Jonathan looked up when she did not respond, and searched her face for comprehension. "The derrière." His Texas drawl made the word sound more like three words - dare e air. The *air* portion hung there awkwardly.

Kat refused to let this moment pass too quickly, but this last word was almost too much for her to restrain her amusement at his discomfort. Where had he learned such a word, she wondered. She waited to see what further creative description he could pull from his vocabulary.

His face worked. A line creased the space between his eyebrows. "His backside." He made a vague wave of his hand in the direction of his hips.

"Oh! You must be trying to tell me he was injured in his buttocks."

His lips drew a thin line across his face. "Yes, ma'am."

"You might have simply told me that."

Kat was fairly certain she saw the tug of a smile at the corners of his eyes.

"I'll get my bag."

"But it's late, Dr. Meriwether. It's a bit of a ride up to the cabin. You'd be coming back in the dark I imagine. I'm sure we can wait for him."

She turned and looked at him, noticing for the first time how unusually dark his eyes were, a shade of gray, shaded by black lashes.

"I'm not sure your father would approve," he said.

Kat lifted an eyebrow at that. "Mister...," she paused, "Winthrop, yes?"

Jonathan nodded.

"Mr. Winthrop, I stopped needing my father's approval quite a few years ago." She turned on her heel and walked into the office feeling a most unbecoming sense of satisfaction at having the last word.

Kat didn't bother to change out of her pants, but pulled on her leather jacket for the return ride, anticipating a drop in temperature. She also changed into her riding boots and shoved her father's hat on her head, her long braid draped over one shoulder. After securing her bag to the Morgan, she pulled herself into the saddle. Jonathan led the way down the hill, through town and beyond toward the foothills.

After following him for a while, she let Blue catch up to Jonathan's horse, falling in beside him on the wide trail that skirted the river. "So where is your ranch? I grew up here and know the area fairly well."

"Timothy and his son, the boy you saw me with last week, have settled in a place the locals call Schmidt's Valley."

She checked the frown before he could see it.

"You know it?" he asked.

"I do. I used to spend quite a bit of time up there when I was young."

"Hmm. It's mighty pretty right now. I think it'll be a good spread for them."

Kat grew quiet. She felt the jealousy of familiarity, and a touch of mourning for the lost solitude of her valley. A narrowing of the trail gave her an excuse to drop behind Jonathan's bay.

She watched the tilt of his shoulders as they swayed in rhythm with his horse's gait. Relaxed heels, easy poise, and gentle hands all bespoke a lifetime of equine companionship. A man could spend every year of his life in a saddle and not have that natural kinship that he betrayed with every softly murmured, "Ho, there," or near invisible cue of his knees or heels. As she watched the mostly silent dialog that constantly flows between a good horseman and his partner, she felt the edge of her jealousy wane. There could be worse people to call her valley home.

Kat found the trail grow more familiar, gentle switchbacks taking them to the higher elevation with open vistas at each turn to the valley floor. Kat's Morgan seemed impatient with the bay's slow pace and she had to rein her in from attempting to pass on the narrow trail. At one point the bay huffed her disapproval, lifting her hind quarters in a low hop, just a hint of warning. Jonathan chuckled softly and checked her attitude with a feather light twitch of the reins.

"Easy, Jessie." Jonathan glanced back over his shoulder, giving Kat's smaller mare a closer look. "She's an uncommon breed to find out here, a little flashier than I'm used to seeing. A morgan, right?"

"Yes. My father gave her to me."

"What is she? Fifteen hands? She couldn't be much more, I'm thinking."

"Fifteen and two inches."

"She's a sturdy little thing, even if she does have some flash." He turned his head back to the trail.

Oddly, she could think of nothing more to say, but felt a bit offended by his suggestion that her roan mare was flashy. The description seemed like disapproval. She was lively, and liked to step out, but *flashy*?

She hadn't noticed before just how broad his shoulders were. The jacket, stretched tight across his back, did little to hide the bulge of his biceps. She calculated that most of his weight must come from lean muscle. As her eyes moved up from his shoulders to the thick cords of his neck, she argued with herself that her interest was nothing more than clinical. Abruptly, she pulled herself back from such thoughts and she sat up straighter, pulling brutally at her ear until she winced with the pain.

Thankfully, they broke from the tree line into the open grassland before she could inflict any more pain on herself. Rays of afternoon sun still warmed the valley floor. Smoke curled from the chimney and the boy stepped out onto the porch at the sound of their approach. He grinned broadly at Kat as he took hold of Blue's reins. "I'll tie her for you."

The lead in his hands, Adam slipped to the other side of Jonathan and whispered, "Father isn't going to be too happy about this."

Jonathan stepped down and handed his reins to Adam. "I suppose not, but his back end won't care in the long run."

Adam snickered at that and walked both horses over to the water trough.

Timothy was lying on his stomach in the far corner of the room. He looked up at Kat and groaned. Kat wasn't sure if it was because he'd seen that she was a woman or that he had just experienced a stab of pain. She was fairly certain it was the former.

"Dr. Meriwether this is Timothy Hindricks. Timothy?" Jonathan waited for Timothy to lift his head to look at them. At last, he did and gave her a thin smile to cover his embarrassment.

Jonathan wore an apologetic expression. "Timothy, this is Dr. Meriwether."

"Didn't know there were two of you," the big man said.

Kat laughed lightly. "Well, there's just the one of me. If you're referring to my father, he was out on another call. I think I can help if you'll let me."

Timothy let out a heavy sigh and dropped his face to the pillow again. The voice came to them muffled, "Guess, I don't have much of a choice."

"No, I don't suppose you do." With that she pulled her bag to the side of the bed. "I'm sorry, but you'll have to remove your trousers."

The muffled groan came from somewhere in the depths of the pillow again. "Not as sorry as me."

Adam passed the plate of beans and ham to Kat as she sat down at the table. She wondered if his gleeful manner was the result of what he saw as his father's humorous situation or that she'd agreed to stay for dinner. Jonathan passed her a plate of cornbread. She had to admit to herself that she was ravenous. The aromas of Timothy's meal that he'd prepared - before the encounter with the mule - had made a compelling argument to stay.

"My father is a *really* good cook, Dr. Meriwether." Adam beamed at her as he handed her a bowl of honey.

"If anything tastes as good as it smells, I'm certain I'll agree with you, Adam."

For long moments, the three ate in silence. Both Kat and Jonathan spoke at once. Jonathan nodded to Kat to continue.

"I was just wondering when you arrived in the valley?" she asked.

Jonathan glanced at Adam before answering. "We moved a few dozen head of cattle out of Utah Territory last fall. Adam and his father plan to homestead here."

Kat gave Adam a warm smile and said, "I've known this valley a long time. It's lovely here. Summers, the floor will open up like a blue carpet with wildflowers. You know that there used to be a family of beavers at the far end of the valley near the white granite outcropping. In less than two years they turned that end into a marsh of meandering streams and little islands. And whole flocks of swan come in the fall to make their winter home here." She looked up to see both men looking at her strangely.

"As I said, I used to come here often as a girl." She took a bite of cornbread, grateful to give her mouth something to do other than blather.

"Sounds real pretty," Jonathan said after a moment. Kat felt those gray eyes on her and studiously remained focused on the plate in front of her. "There was a place in east Texas that I used to know as a boy on my father's ranch. It was special too."

He didn't elaborate. He seemed to have offered it up to ease her discomfort. She was grateful.

"And what about you, Mr. Winthrop? Are you planning to stay here?"

Jonathan, his mouth still full of cornbread, seemed to use the time chewing to consider his answer. "Well, I promised the boy and his father to help them get the place fit for next winter. After that, I'm not sure. I've ruminated a bit about Oregon."

"I see." Kat stabbed at a piece of ham and wondered why his answer bothered her. Wasn't Idaho Territory good enough?

"Make sure you thank your father for dinner, and help him change that dressing daily for the first week. If you need help, send word. However, I think he'll be very cooperative with you, if the alternative means that I return." She caught Jonathan's eye and neither one of them could restrain a knowing grin.

As she gathered her bag and pulled on her jacket, Jonathan reached for his hat. She anticipated his offer to accompany her back to town and held up a hand. "Mr. Winthrop, I'll be fine on my own. Remember, I know this valley. I know the trail."

Jonathan looked down at her, his hat still in his hand. "I'm not sure I can let you go alone."

There was something in the way he phrased it that gave her pause, something authoritative in his voice. She felt he'd said those words before with an expectation of compliance.

"Really! I insist that you stay with Timothy. He needs your attention more than I." With that declaration, she walked to the door without giving him time to protest.

Jonathan stood on the porch with Adam at his side, watching as she mounted up on the little roan. She looked back at them and reached down to pat the leather scabbard on her saddle and the butt end of the Browning Rifle. "I'm a very good shot, Mr. Winthrop."

She was a bit surprised that he'd not protested more. A secret part of her, squashed down and stuffed in a corner, was even a little sorry for it. Kat nudged her mare with her knees and started off at a fast trot down the trail.

"Certainly knows her own mind, don't she?" Adam mused.

"Hmm. Not so sure of that, but she's headstrong for certain." There was no condemnation in his words.

The waxing moon provided a small degree of illumination to the trail, but even without it, she'd have known the way. The little Morgan's sure-footed breeding made her an excellent trail horse. She reached down and slipped her hand beneath Blue's black mane, patting her neck.

"Blue, you're a prize, for sure." *Flashy, indeed*! She scowled into the night.

Passing beneath a fragrant canopy of pine, she heard the rustling of wings above her. She glanced up in time to see a stirring of white against the black outline of branches. An owl screeched off into the evening air, offended by their intrusion. At each sound, she jumped. It wasn't like her and she chastised herself for her anxiety.

Halfway down the trail she'd climbed earlier with Jonathan, she turned Blue's head to a smaller animal trail that she had long known as a shortcut leading to her family's small parcel of land above the town. But behind the entry still concealed from the main trail, the path looked as if it had seen some recent use. The grass was trampled and overhanging brush revealed broken branches at rider height.

To her right, the sudden rustling in a tangle of wild black-berry bushes made her startle again. With a thrill, she remembered the delicious fright of night sounds that had brought her time and again onto mountain trails on moonlit nights. How she'd missed this in the cloistered setting of the city, where nighttime sounds were the angered yowling of cat fights and baleful barking of dogs! So why was she acting like a school girl jumping at the very sounds she had grown to love?

From up ahead there came a sound of something that did-n't belong. She pulled up on Blue's reins and waited, straining to hear it again. It was a voice, and not far ahead. Some instinct directed her to pull the Morgan well off the trail and into the cover of low branches. She slipped from the saddle and lay her hand gently on Blue's muzzle, willing her to be quiet.

There were two voices, one gruff and one higher in tim-bre and somewhat familiar. She waited as they drew nearer, her heart pounding in her ears. Certain they would hear it, she held her breath. She heard a curse from one, and then their indistinct conversation ceased as they walked within a few feet of where she stood, hidden by the damp, the boughs, and the night. The smaller man pulled up his horse and turned toward her. He swung his head to look back down the trail, and as he did, she recognized the chiseled face of Ethan Hall. Even in the faint light, she was certain it was him.

The gruff voice spoke, "What's wrong?"

"I thought I heard someone behind us," Ethan replied.

"You're just spooked. There ain't nobody back there. You got no more backbone than a slug."

Ethan spun around and kicked his horse into a trot, ignoring the man's taunt. The voice of the bigger man who had spoken, also sounded vaguely familiar, but his hat created an even deeper shadow over his face.

Kat stayed where she was for long moments, until she could no longer hear their horses' footsteps. She stepped from her cover and looked back the way they had come. Why had they been here? And why was Ethan worried about being followed?

She stepped into the stirrup and pulled herself up into the saddle again. "Come on, Blue. This mountain is just a little too crowded for me." With a light kick of her heel, the morgan sprang off at a quick pace.

At a switchback behind Kat, where the trail forked, the men pulled up. The man she had not identified took the saddlebag passed to him by Ethan. The larger man's horse skittered to the side as the saddlebag thumped against its side.

From his concealed position, Jonathan watched the interchange. He didn't need to hear their words to discern the tension between them, their tones harsh and clipped. He remained hidden until the two men split company, one heading up the mountain, the other heading back down the main trail to town.

Leading Jessie back to the trail, Jonathan knelt at the place the two men had just occupied, his hand moving over the tracks like a divining rod looking for water. The tracks confirmed his observation. Those packs they'd been carrying were heavy. Scanning the trail below him he could still make out Kat and the Morgan now back on the visible portion of the trail. He'd been impressed at her instincts to step out of sight of the unknown riders. There was something more to the girl than a head full of book education. Somewhere along the way she'd learned some practical knowledge of self-preservation.

He stored that information along with what he'd gleaned from the men who'd just passed. Pulling himself back into the saddle, he continued quietly down the trail always with Kat just ahead and always in sight.

Old habits die hard. The habits of a Ranger had developed in him a suspicious mind, a trait that had allowed him to survive when others had not. He read people, measuring words as other people might assess a person's height or weight, and he rarely trusted anyone to be completely honest. Years as a lawman had taught him that nearly everyone had secrets buried in dark places, sometimes very ugly, dark places.

This town most certainly was hiding some. Although he'd determined that it was no longer his job to uncover them, he couldn't stand by and let harm come to the girl when she'd done him a favor by coming to the mountain cabin. His years of habit acting as a protector, required he do this - to see her safely home. It was who he was, a part of himself that he couldn't put away as easily as his Winchester or unpinning his Ranger star.

Dual Suspicions

WHAT DO YOU think, Kat?"

At the mention of her name, Kat sat up straighter. She hadn't been listening, her mind drifting to a place far from the stuffy drawing room and colorful assembly of Snowberry's most respectable women. She'd gone to that far-away place in a desperate attempt to save her mind from becoming a mush pot as she listened to the senseless bickering about tablecloth colors and contest rules for baked goods.

Their hostess, Victoria Townsend, repeated her question with an edge of irritation coloring it. "Dr. Kat what do you think about changing the baking contest from cake to pie? We've had cake contests for four years in a row! I think it's time we get ourselves out of this rut!"

Kat looked blankly back at the woman's flushed cheeks and thin lips. All she could muster was a flat, "I like pie."

"Well, see? There it is! Dr. Kat's in favor." She waved her hand like a flapping fish out of water. "I move that we hold a pie baking contest this year."

Mrs. Forester raised her hand. "I suppose a change might be in order. Takes less flour to bake a pie anyway. I'll second the motion." Kat lifted a skeptical eyebrow at that reasoning.

Four women voted for the change, three against. Some heavy sighs and murmuring followed before Mrs. Forester wisely suggested it was time for refreshments.

Before they'd finished their cake and tea, Kat had been *elected* to oversee the contest. It happened so fast, she'd had no opportunity to even protest or contrive some plausible excuse. When she realized that the appointment to judge spared her from entering any cooking contests, she experienced some small degree of relief and counted herself lucky to have gotten off with such a light sentence.

Kat stayed to help clean up and found herself at the sink with Mrs. Forester.

"Well, that went well, considering," Mrs. Forester said with a definite tone of sarcasm.

Kat glanced over at her. "Considering what?"

"That Hermione Schuster has won the baking contest three years in a row, and Victoria has never won even runner up. They both consider themselves expert cooks and haven't spoken to each other since last year's picnic."

"Oh," Kat inserted with minimal understanding.

"Last year they both entered with a chiffon cake that looked and tasted surprisingly similar. They each accused the other of stealing the recipe. So that year, neither won, because the judges couldn't decide between two identical cakes, so they chose Nathan McAllister's rum cake instead. The judges were quite enthusiastic to award the prize to him, and for the first time there were no leftovers. Nathan took home the prize and an empty plate."

None too gently, Kat poked her elbow into Mrs. Forester's arm. "And you! You dropped me right into the whole mess!"

The older woman shrugged. "Someone had to break the tie. It was the easiest way and I knew it would draw the least amount of blood." She sniggered in a very unladylike manner.

"You're quite the manipulator, aren't you?" Kat said and chuckled at the thought of the two women locked in combat, hair askew, skirts over their dimpled knees, fingernails digging tracks into each other's faces.

Mrs. Forester and Kat left Mrs. Townsend's house together, Kat promising to review the rules for the contest next week. Mrs. Townsend reminded her emphatically that there would need to be some modifications to allow for the change in confection. Kat successfully managed not to roll her eyes.

"Won't you come in for a cup of tea? I have a fitting for Chelsea Hawthorn at two, but we could visit a spell." Mrs. Forester and Kat stood on the boardwalk outside her store.

"I'd love to, but I need to check in at the office to see if Father needs help. I've been filling in for him when he rides out to do home visits."

"Well, I'm certain he appreciates the help. He's been mighty busy. We've missed seeing Jacob at services on Sunday."

Kat failed to hide her surprise and gave a bark of laughter. "Father?"

"Oh, I know. He didn't want to have much to do with religion after your mama passed on, but he has been coming. Doesn't say much. Doesn't stay long after, always in a hurry to get back to the office. But for the past year or so, he's been quite regular."

"Father." She stated it again, leaving off the questioning tone and making it a statement of affirmation as if to picture it more clearly, this unlikely description of her agnostic father.

Mrs. Forester laughed at her disbelief. "Yes, your father. Don't look so stunned. God can call even the most stubborn heart. I should know!"

Kat raised her eyebrows another centimeter, then shook her head. "It's just not something I'd ever have expected of him. He's always been a man of science, not believing anything he can't test or see with his own eyes."

With a bemused expression, Mrs. Forester placed her hand on Kat's arm. "A lot has changed since you've been gone, dear. As we get older, life has a way of changing our perspectives. Your papa has had a lot of time to himself since you've been away, time to think about what's on the other side of this." She waved her hand vaguely, taking in the town, the land, the sky.

She turned to the door. "You know, we're having a pot-luck this Sunday and I'd love to show you off to some new folks in town, even if you are a heathen."

Kat threw back her head and laughed. "Well, I'll certainly ask father tonight at dinner. I suspect this will give rise to an interesting conversation."

She picked up the edge of her skirt and turned to step into the road, nearly colliding with Ethan Hall *again*. Giving him a hard smile, she stepped back. "Mr. Hall."

"How fortunate we are to have run into you again," Ethan said with a smooth smile gliding across his chiseled features.

At the same time as he said "we" she noticed the older man to his side.

"Let me introduce my father, Dr. Meriwether. This is--"

"Gilford Hall, ma'am," Hall interrupted, stepping forward and thrusting a beefy hand at her.

Ethan stepped back as easily as any military subordinate might have. She discerned in that telling moment something of their relationship. Ethan's easy smile slipped from his face just as he had slipped into the background. For just an instant, she felt a little sorry for the son as she saw him in contrast to his father. Ethan, she surmised, lived in the shadow.

"It is a pleasure to meet you, Dr. Meriwether. Snowberry is very fortunate to have two doctors in our humble town." The words seemed to slide from his lips like butter off a hot knife.

His ingratiating manner immediately fanned a flare of resentment - the way he referred to Snowberry as *our* town as if he could claim some right to ownership after such a short time. Before she could moderate her reaction, she said, "My father has served here for over twelve years now. I think he's done quite well on his own." With a lift of her eyebrow and coy tilt of her head she asked, "How long have you been here, Mr. Hall?"

His jaw tightened involuntarily, giving her a thrill of satisfaction to know he'd understood the message perfectly. The next moment she derided herself for yielding to such adolescent verbal sparring. Why should it matter that the man was so full of himself? But it *did* matter if innocent people were being harmed because of his ineptitude.

"Oh, I'm a recently relocated immigrant, for sure, ma'am. But I've come to treasure this community, all the good decent folks who just want to make a peaceful life for themselves. That's why I felt compelled to offer my experience as a lawman to keep this valley secure."

"It's strange that there seems to be more violence in our valley since I left." Kat folded her hands in front of her, standing rigid. She couldn't help but notice that Ethan studiously avoided eye contact with her.

"Well, there's the pity, isn't it? I could see it coming when more men moved into the mining camps up north. They're a hard sort, some violent. Those that don't make a strike often as not, turn to thievery." He rocked back on his heels, squinting at her with a hard smile. "That's why I knew there was no time to lose. They needed my help. I just couldn't stand by and watch a good town full of good people suffer."

"And have you made any progress in locating the men responsible for this most recent attack?" Kat wondered if the man was anything more than a braggart, or if he had indeed been a lawman. Had anyone even asked him if he had any experience to qualify him as sheriff?

"Well, I'm glad you asked, 'cause just this morning I sent word requesting additional help in patrolling the road. There's a very talented man that I know who has been very successful stopping this sort of trouble."

Kat caught the sudden stiffening of Ethan's body, the remnants of his smile evaporating.

She had no desire to continue the discussion, finding it more difficult to restrain her irritation with the man's smugness. Knowing her temper, she'd avoid shaming her father by causing an unpleasant scene. It was high time she extricated herself from this most unpleasant first meeting and get herself on home before she said, or did something regretful. "Well, it's good to hear that you understand the severity of our problem. I'm sure you've taken steps to ensure the town's safety. Now, if you'll excuse me, I need to return to the office. My father will be expecting me."

With that, she stepped to the side, walking rapidly away before he could say more.

Gilford Hall turned slowly, watching her go, his eyes narrowing to slits while his mouth widened into a predatory smile. "That girl's got spunk. Think I like her."

He threw a glance at Ethan. "If I were your age, I'd be on that girl's tail like a dog in heat." Hall's face stretched wide with a leering grin.

Ethan closed his eyes, wishing he could likewise close his ears to the vulgarity of his father's opinions. He too, watched her go, but with a growing concern. Her coolness toward his father set off clanging alarms in his head. She knew something. She suspected something. That suspicion might create an unpleasant situation he had no desire to deal with, but might have no way to avoid.

A Rumble of Thunder

"YES, WE ARE going fishing and no arguments!" Using her cutting knife like a pointing finger, Kat looked up from the kitchen counter to throw her father a warning glare.

"But Kat, Josie might deliver any day. I usually visit Will on Wednesday and see how he's managing without Irma around. I mean what if something happens?" Her father stood with arms folded watching her pack generous slices of fresh bread and a large wedge of cheese into her saddlebag.

"Papa, you'll do what you always do when you go out on calls. You'll tell Mr. Forester where you'll be. If an emergency arises, he'll know how to send folks to find you." She turned to him with her hands resolutely braced on her hips. "But only if it's life threatening!"

Looking about the office uncertainly, but noting the stubborn stance of his only daughter, Nathaniel rubbed the back of his neck. "I don't know."

Kat, closing the flap on her saddlebag, stepped to her father's side and took a firm grasp of his arm. "I do. We're going."

Nathaniel allowed her to tow him out the door, but not without one more weak argument, "But I'm not even sure I know where all my gear is!"

"I do!" As they stepped outside, she gestured to the basket already tied to her father's gelding. Two poles rose high like knight standards where she'd lashed them to the saddle. "I've already taken care of it. Now let's go! You always told me the best fish don't wait for any man."

They rode quickly down the hill to the Foresters' door where Kat hopped down to stick a note between the frame and the door with instructions about where to find them. At the west end of town where the newest houses stood, they began the gradual climb to the foothills. Here the Payette River spread out for a mile or so where two smaller streams fed into it, one with colder waters than the other. It was along the shore of the colder stream that Kat directed Blue.

The stream rose gradually from the valley floor, snowberry and wild lilac bushes giving way to a few scattered pines. A cottonwood loomed before them as they rounded a low hill. On the opposite bank rose a pile of jagged granite boulders, looking as if they'd been intentionally stockpiled there by some passing troll. Here the stream lingered on its journey to the river, forming a deep still pool. Their favorite fishing hole looked just as she'd remembered it. What a relief that at least this one thing had not changed in her absence.

Wasting no time, she slid out of the saddle. Blue eagerly set to grazing while she spread out a quilt on the new spring grass a few feet from the stream. With a deep sigh, Kat plopped down, flung her arms wide and fell back on the blanket, supremely satisfied with this moment.

Forgetting his earlier reluctance, Nathaniel, accepting the challenge of the fishing hole, searched eagerly through his bag for just the right hook. Meanwhile, a sassy trout taunted him as it swam in lazy patterns around boulders and under shady overhanging limbs.

Kat breathed deeply of the damp awakening earth before propping her head on her hand. Seeing her father wholeheartedly engaged in a leisurely pastime rather than elbow deep in someone's bloody problems - it filled her heart with gladness. "When was the last time you came out here, Papa?"

He straightened, cocking his head to the side, thinking. "Probably the summer before you left for Boston."

Kat clucked her disapproval. "All work and no play, Papa."

"Stop talking and let me fish!"

She pulled out the book she'd been unsuccessfully trying to read, making no more headway than the first ten pages in almost as many months. Today would be different.

Ten minutes later she slammed the book shut and sat up. She jumped to her feet and glanced at her father, intent on baiting his hook. Without disturbing him, she started up the narrow animal trail along the stream. Every few feet she found it necessary to duck her head to pass beneath low branches. At least, she thought, the thorny berry bushes were mostly contained to the opposite bank.

The terrain altered, the vegetation becoming less dense the farther she traveled. She found she could walk without bending over. She stopped, straining to hear what she expected. A few yards farther the sound of falling water increased. Kat smiled, quickening her pace.

A few feet from the stream, the bank rose steeply. Squeezed into a narrow fissure, water cascaded down the face of moss-covered rock. A shallow pool carved out of weathered limestone lay at its base. From the cloven rock, ferns sprouted in riotous fashion. It was a fairytale world that had for years belonged to her alone.

She knelt then at the mossy lip of the pool and looked down. What fantasies she had created here as a child, of talking rabbits and enchanted birds that whispered their secret identities in her ear! She had known then that had she the courage to fall into the pool, she too would be transformed. But she did not then attempt it nor did she now.

She sat back on her heels, hands caressing the velvet moss. *Choices.* Life was a series of choices, some hard, some easy. As a child, they were things like, *pretend ponies or sheriffs? Eat the mud pie or don't? Obey or disobey?* For most of her adulthood, it seemed her choices always boiled down to *stay or go.* Stay in Snowberry, or go to school? Beg her suitor to stay, and leave her scholastic dreams behind? *Stay or go. Go or stay.* Why did it keep coming back to these two rending choices? How to know if she had chosen wisely? Was she choosing wisely now? And the *what ifs* began to parade before her. The one that loomed the largest, the elephant in the parade, was yet to be decided. What if she didn't take the position in San Francisco? What if she gave up the dream? Was there another to replace it?

The trail climbed from here to a ridge with a vista of the river behind her. Relieved that she'd chosen to wear trousers, she scrambled over the rocks, beginning to climb. It wasn't particularly far, but there was no trail to follow, so she had to pick her way through the brush around some rocky outcroppings. As her hands scraped on rough stones, she regretted not wearing her riding gloves.

At last she emerged from the thick underbrush and ducking under the branches of a low-hanging cedar, she found herself looking out over the valley to the south and west. Shading her eyes, she peered in the direction of the town. Looking more like a storybook village from this height, the effect of white-washed cottages and small businesses arrayed in orderly symmetry charmed her. Kat found her favorite ledge, one she was certain was created just for her with a flat seat and a short back to lean against. She perched on the rock, hugging her knees to her chest, her chin resting on her knees, sighing with contentment.

"Pretty, ain't it?"

She jerked her head around, a gasp escaping her lips. "Oh!" It was all she said when she saw him.

"I'm sorry, ma'am. I didn't know how to keep from startling you." Jonathan stood a few feet back leaning against a gnarled cedar tree, his arms folded easily across his chest, his hat tipped low shadowing his face.

She experienced a violent transformation in her emotions from absolute serenity to extreme annoyance, as again her private space had been violated. But Jonathan seemed far more interested in the view than in her, so she relaxed as her emotions leveled out again.

Kat remembered then the trail that led from Schmidt's Valley up to the ridge, one she'd taken often, easier than the one she'd just climbed. He must have ridden up from there. She looked up at Jonathan uncertain as to what to say, so she turned her gaze as he had, back to the valley.

Neither spoke for long minutes. The vista held them there, the sinuous curves of the wide green river winding through spring fresh grasses, the patchwork quilt of a town, the layered range of foothills giving way to distant mountains on two sides of the valley. On the far horizon clouds rose in sinister billows of gray and mauve.

"Looks like a storm's comin'." His words, though soft, made the hair on the back of her neck prickle. She kept her eyes trained on the fast approaching bank of angry clouds.

"Yes, it does," she said softly, her voice barely more than a murmur.

"Guess we'd better be gettin' back. This isn't a good place to get caught in a storm, I'd think."

She turned to look at him, his hand stretched out to her. She took it and allowed him to pull her to her feet. With her hand still in his, she heard the first rumblings of thunder as it rolled in across the mountain range before moving across the valley below. The sound prompted her to turn back, seeing gray clouds rolling down from the mountain to cast their shadows over the valley floor. Even now, the air seemed charged with the fierce energy building within them.

"Will you be all right?"

She hesitated, struck by the genuine concern she heard in his voice. But that unpleasant prickle at the base of her neck returned. This was a man of contradictions, she mused. He was a dangerous man, of that she felt certain. She felt, with equal conviction, that she was safer in his company than any place else she'd ever known.

She answered softly, "Yes." Then with more assurance she repeated herself. "Yes, of course."

She felt his eyes upon her as she returned to the trail, knowing that he would stay there until she had begun her descent.

When she emerged from the thicket at the edge of the stream, Nathaniel was waiting with the horses packed and ready to return home. He looked at her anxiously. "You had me worried. That storm's come up fast."

Kat wordlessly took Blue's reins and mounted up.

The storm started with a slow pelting of light rain, but by the time they reached the house it seemed the whole storehouse of heaven had opened.

Nathaniel and Kat stood at the barn door watching the torrent carve shallow canyons in the road to town. Thunder followed in rolls that shook the walls, causing the Morgan to blow and stamp her feet with each clap.

"Haven't seen one like this for quite some time," Nathaniel shouted above the din.

Kat moved closer to her father, hugging his arm. He pulled free of her grip when he felt her shivering. Wrapping his arm around her, he pulled her close. She felt safe again, the same way she had felt secure with Jonathan Winthrop. Aside from her father, she'd never experienced that assurance of protection in anyone else's presence. She wondered at that. Something in his calm manner, his keen watchfulness, his quietly measured speech, all communicated to her that Jonathan was a man of intentionally, restrained strength.

After a time, the space between thunderclaps increased as the storm rolled beyond the valley and into the far blue range. Kat leaned heavily against her father, breathing in the familiar scent of him.

He squeezed her tighter to him. "I used to tell you when you were a little girl and scared that thunder wasn't anything more than two forces of nature meeting head on. As you grew older, I explained a little more about the science of it. Remember?"

Kat looked up and saw that he was seeing something beyond the passing storm, whether in the past or future she wasn't sure. "I remember, Papa. You gave me the science for everything. It made me feel stronger knowing the why of things."

Nathaniel looked down at her. A vague almost puzzled expression washed across his face. "You know that the older I get, the more I realize how little I know. I could still tell you the why. But lately, I've been thinking more about the who."

"Is that why you've been going to church lately?"

Nathaniel laughed lightly. "Should've known the wags would have filled your ear about that. I wasn't sure how you'd react when you learned about it. Some hypocrite I turned out to be." He shook his head slowly, the laughter fading, replaced by that contemplative expression she'd seen earlier. "It's just that there are questions these days I can't answer with science anymore. People that should be dead, who aren't. Remedies I couldn't administer with my entire apothecary couldn't cure them, but they were healed. Things happen that I can't explain."

Nathaniel pulled back and shrugged. "I'm just looking for answers, Kat, just like I always have. But I've pretty much exhausted the places to look for them." He gave her a half smile. "Sometimes, of late, I think I've been asking the wrong questions."

Whispered Warnings

"MRS. GILLET, HIS leg looks very good! I see no inflammation, no evidence of infection." Kat looked up from her examination of Mrs. Gillet's four-year-old son. "The wound is healing nicely."

Kat saw the relief wash over Mrs. Gillet's face as the woman stepped back from where she'd been peering over Kat's shoulder.

"Praise be to God!" she said while fanning her florid face.

Kat heard the catch in her voice, recalling the tragedy of her older son's death. Five years ago, by the time the family had decided to call her father, the gangrene had beset the leg and even amputation couldn't save his life. Such an unnecessary death.

People needed to be educated, she thought for not the first time since returning to the valley. Snake oil salesmen could make all the promises, but the alcohol-laced remedies they sold could do nothing against infection. More of these hardworking people were likely to die, not from their wounds, but from the infection that followed. Her father had made much progress in the years he'd treated the community of Snowberry, but with newer treatments, she knew much more could be done to improve the quality of life here on the frontier.

Mrs. Gillet pulled the corner of her apron to her eye. "I'm so grateful that your father moved here. And now to have two of you, well, it's just wonderful. When Daniel cut his leg with that axe, I just feared the worst, you know? I couldn't bear to think of burying two of my babies before they were growed."

The older woman placed a kettle on the wood stove to boil, talking while she prepared a pot of tea. "You know, I couldn't understand why your papa just didn't bleed Daniel of that infection. But he seemed quite set on not doin' what even my mother would have expected as proper treatment. Had to trust him to know best, him being educated and all. But it surely was hard."

Kat shivered involuntarily as she imagined the horrors of those days, not so long passed, when bleeding a patient was standard practice. Her father's education had taught him the futility and even harm such procedures brought about. She also now knew the strides modern science had made since her father had studied, progress she hoped to share with him in the days ahead.

While she put a fresh bandage on the boy's leg, Kat couldn't help but notice things that confirmed for her the need to educate the townspeople about sanitary handling of food and water. But would they listen? Could they be convinced that these unseen microbes could be the cause of so much suffering?

Kat accepted the cup of tea she'd been offered but declined the bread after seeing that the same knife that had been used to slice the bread had been laying on the counter where it had been obviously used to slice bacon for the morning meal. She hoped she hadn't insulted Mrs. Gillet in the process of protecting her health.

"I'm glad the Picnic Committee ladies decided to change the contest this year. It's about time, if you ask me. We've been watching those two hens, pardon my saying it clear, peck at each other for long enough! Heard you might have had somethin' to do with that." She winked.

"Oh, I hardly think so. To be honest, I don't even remember casting a vote," Kat said.

"You sure you won't have a slice of bread? I made it fresh this mornin'. You could sample my Thimbleberry jam. I'm plannin' to enter it this year." Mrs. Gillet sat across from Kat and rubbed her glistening brow with the hem of her apron.

Kat looked down at her teacup. "Thank you, Mrs. Gillet. I had quite a breakfast just before I rode over."

Mrs. Gillet sat back, folding her hands across her ample chest. "Your father has done for himself quite well since your ma passed on. From what I hear, he should enter one of the cooking contests!"

It came as no surprise that even Nathaniel Meriwether's private talents might be common knowledge among the wags of their small town. "Well, I'll tell him you threw out the challenge then." She laughed lightly.

Kat could see from Mrs. Gillet's eager eyes that she was braced for a stimulating conversation. Kat wasn't sure she was ready to be broadcasting any gossip. It would definitely be in the category of "unprofessional behavior" amongst her colleagues in Boston.

Mrs. Gillet must have sensed Kat's imminent departure, leaning forward she said, "It's sure a shame about these robberies. And to think they're taking place right across the valley. Here! In our own little Snowberry!" She shook her head, *tsking* through tight lips.

"Indeed, it is." With this Kat could agree.

"You know what I think? We need a real lawman. That's what I think." She sat back, folding her hands across her chest again.

Kat, while she abhorred the idea that her town had been infected by gold and silver fever which might necessitate any law enforcement, had to agree again. She also doubted that anyone would want such a job. Most of the townspeople were far too busy trying to scrape out a living to take on another job.

"Have any of the businessmen in town looked into hiring anyone other than Mr. Hall?" Kat asked.

"Hardly think so. Hall, he hardly takes anything for doin' what he does. Whatever that is." Mrs. Gillet wagged her head, *tsking* again with greater emphasis.

"I see."

"But you know what I think?" Mrs. Gillet leaned forward, one eyebrow cocked.

Kat knew this to be another rhetorical question so she waited.

"I think someone should go up to Schmidt's Valley and ask that fella that moved into the old homestead. Cause I heard he was a Texas Ranger! Imagine that! Now that there's a real lawman! I suppose he'd set things right." Mrs. Gillet sat back looking pleased with her solution.

Kat tried to picture the quiet man with the shielded, dark eyes as a lawman. The image didn't fit, and seemed quite contrary to her initial impression of him. He seemed too kind and reserved to have come from such a violent past. Then again, there was that dangerous element she'd sensed, but more than likely this was just one more example of Mrs. Gillet's active imagination.

"Well, perhaps if Mr. Hall takes his job seriously, he'll hire more professional lawmen to patrol the road." Kat quickly finished her tea, rising to her feet before Mrs. Gillet could take the gossip any further. "Thank you for the tea, Mrs. Gillet. Either my father or I will be out to remove the stitches from Daniel's leg next week."

Mrs. Gillet sent her off with a full loaf of bread wrapped in a somewhat clean cloth, shouting her gratitude again as Kat took her leave.

Kat rode from the Gillet homestead keenly aware of the civilized world she'd left behind in Boston, marveling at the vastly different life she'd returned to here in her hometown. It seemed more than distance that separated these two worlds. In many ways, she felt as if she'd stepped from the future into the past, not just her own, but that somehow time had actually reversed when she'd boarded the train in Boston. Somewhere between the bustling cities of New England and the border of Idaho Territory she'd passed through a portal in time, where the world of policemen and modern innovations dissolved to this outpost of vigilantes and superstition.

Perhaps it was her heaviness of heart that led her to take the fork in the road leading back to Schmidt's Meadow. The farther from the Gillet homestead and town she traveled, the lighter rose her spirits. Blue stepped out at a brisk trot, head held high. Instead of taking the main trail to the valley, she took the narrow trail that led higher up the high mountain valley. She gave into her curiosity to see if anyone had discovered the older trapper's cabin on the side of Mt. Baldy.

When she'd last seen it, the ancient structure was a spooky old place with sinking roof and gaping holes in the floorboards. The stone fireplace alone seemed to be propping up the rest of the cabin. Only once had she and Josie dared to venture inside, and that was only because of a sudden thunderstorm which had taken them by surprise. It had been a balmy spring day until the skies had bruised, growing heavy with an unexpected storm. The cabin had provided the only safe shelter in an area of several miles. Inside they'd found a half-dozen cans of food with labels printed in a foreign language. A few pans remained on the shelves, abandoned by the last residents.

The girls had heard stories of the French trappers who had worked in the mountains before the first immigrants blazed the Oregon Trail. But little evidence remained to unravel the mystery of who had built the cabin. Aside from a broken animal trap propped in the corner and the remnants of some moth-eaten animal skin nailed to a wall, little was left to identify those who'd lived there. As they sat in the dusty gloom, thunder rattling the walls and rain dripping through numerous holes in the roof, they had conjured stories of the dastardly outlaws that had holed up in this cabin, imagining how that stain on the floor was the only evidence remaining of a treacherous betrayal between brothers. After the storm had abated and the girls had made their way home, rather more subdued, Kat had slept not a wink. Though they had never spoken of it, she rather suspected that it had been much the same for Josie.

The trail grew narrower and the footing more difficult the higher she and Blue traveled. Kat felt a delightful tingling of anticipation. It had always been this way for her, never one to back down from a fight or to avoid the possibility of an adventure. The more scared Josie was by a proposed adventure, the more resolute Kat was to pursue it.

She dismounted when she thought she was close, leading the Morgan through the dense vegetation encroaching on the trail. Stepping into the clearing, she could see that twining berries had reclaimed a large portion of the cleared area behind the cabin. The structure itself was half consumed by dense woody vines and years of accumulated leaves.

As much as the cabin still resembled the haunted shack she remembered, there was something out of place. Standing in the shadowed edge of the woodland, she held Blue's reins tightly in her hand while surveying the area. The roof dipped at a crazy angle where a tree limb had grown down to rest wearily upon a corner. With each year's growth the roof had borne a little more of its weight.

That's when she noticed that the door was unnaturally clear of the vines covering most of the cabin. Someone had cut away an opening, allowing the door to be functional once again. Odd, she thought. Then she remembered the men who had taken possession of the Schmidt homestead. Perhaps they'd come up here and decided to investigate the cabin. She frowned to think of yet one more sanctuary intruded upon.

Hidden in the shade, she scanned the area before crossing the open area and approaching the cabin. Dropping Blue's reins, she stepped onto the porch. The door, warped by the weathering of years, would not fully close so she nudged it open with her shoulder. A creaking protest of iron on rusted iron announced her presence. Cringing at the sound, she peered into the room, lit only by a few narrow rays of light streaming through cracks in the walls and the half-open doorway.

As her eyes adjusted, she stepped a bit farther into the room. Her toe kicked an empty can that went clattering across the floor. Her heart nearly leapt out of her chest. Although the cabin was dirty with cobwebs and rat droppings, the counter and crude table had been wiped clean of dust. Cans with new labels lined the shelf by the sink. Two pallets with blankets took a good portion of the floor space on either side of the ancient rock fireplace. Someone was definitely making themselves a home here. Frowning she stepped back onto the porch.

Why would anyone want to live this high on the mountain? There was no evidence of mining. Maybe they were just drifters, skirting the towns where they might encounter unwanted questions. Her curiosity stirred, leading her to investigate the surrounding area. One thing she felt confident of was that there had been at least three different horses here in recent weeks. The tracks were distinct.

She shook her head, chiding herself for her childlike imagination. There could be any number of reasons, men might avoid civilized settlements. But she couldn't shake the thought that the location would make a great hideout for those attacking the ore wagons. Even if she were correct, who could she trust with the discovery? Apparently, not Hall. She could see no evidence, no boxes of ore, no gold. All she had was a twist in her gut and a nagging suspicion.

With a petulant expression clouding her face, she swung into the saddle. "Come on, Blue! Let's head back. No reason to stay here." The Morgan tossed her head as though in agreement.

They descended as they'd come up the mountain, staying to the narrow trail rather than taking the fork that would have led them through Schmidt's Meadow. Having no desire to have to explain her presence to either Jonathan Winthrop or

Timothy Hindricks, she and Blue took their time navigating the rocky terrain and finally hooking up with the main trail back to town.

This had proven to be a most unsatisfying day and she found herself completely out of sorts. So, when she saw a horse and rider approaching, she stiffened. In no mood for any social interchange, civil or otherwise, she urged Blue on to a faster pace.

A broad-brimmed hat covered in a heavy layer of dust and grime shadowed the man's whiskered face. She noticed that the horse he rode looked far too small for the man's bulk. When he was within hailing distance, he raised his head to look directly at her. Kat recognized him in an instant, the small malevolent eyes and the nose, bent and broken from the blow she'd delivered those many years ago.

Liam apparently recognized her at the same time, the right side of his mouth pulling up into an appalling attempt at a smile. "Well, I'll be! Kat Meriwether! I'd heard you were back."

Kat nodded to him and said simply, "Liam." She considered riding on by without entering into a dialog with him. But Liam had pulled up his horse and turned its head just enough to block the trail and her ability to walk on.

"I was really hopin' to see you before you left us again." He pushed his hat up with a grubby finger, peering intently at her.

Kat lifted an eyebrow, just a degree, at that remark. Why would he want to see her? And why was he the only one who hadn't assumed she was staying? That question presented the greater puzzle. "I didn't know that I was going anywhere." She heard the terse tone of her own voice, regretting it instantly. Knowing that it would be too easy to fall into their old pattern of verbal sparring, she reminded herself to control her tongue.

Liam pulled the corner of his mouth a degree higher, managing an unpleasant sneer instead of a smile. "Well, I guess it's just I didn't figure that you'd be comin' back to stay here after schoolin' and all." He chuckled and scratched his whiskered chin while keeping his eyes intently focused on her face. "Hey! If you're plannin' on hangin' around, well that's just fine." His horse took an impatient step forward. Liam checked her harshly. "I know we never got along much as kids."

"No. We didn't." It was all she could say. Her mood just wouldn't allow her brain to come up with any socially acceptable response to an obvious statement. Impatience with this unfortunate meeting was growing and she felt her reserve slipping. All she wanted to do was touch a heel to Blue and let her speed home where she could take a long, soothing bath.

"Well, I just want to say that I ain't holdin' no hard feelings. I'm real glad you made yourself somethin' for people to respect around here." His face worked hard to hold his crooked smile in place.

"That's very good of you, Liam," Kat said through tight lips. *Good Lord!* The man was still as irritating as ever. She imagined punching him in the nose again, feeling the cartilage give way beneath her knuckles. That mental picture gave her a moment of pleasure, unfitting for a lady.

Liam inched his horse closer to Blue, still managing to block the trail. "I also gotta say, you're lookin' mighty fine. You turned out to be quite the lady."

By way of response, Kat sat rigid in the saddle, her grip on the reins blanching the knuckles of her left hand. The pleasurable images were suddenly replaced by a quiver of fear as she realized that they weren't kids anymore, her days of thumping bullies clearly over.

"But I also want you to know that I'm a changed man. I ain't the boy I used to be." Liam sat back in the saddle, affecting a relaxed attitude. "So, I'm just hopin' we can bury the hatchet. You know?"

Kat didn't know if she was successfully hiding her skepticism at this confession of transformation. Nothing aside from his sticky words supported his claim. But she knew that the best way to end the conversation civilly would be to accept him at his word.

"Well, I'm very glad to hear that, Liam. I'm sure we'll see each other again." With that, she nudged Blue. The little mare jumped forward, startling Liam's nervous horse off the trail.

Liam called after her, "You know there've been a lot of bad things happening around here lately. You might want to reconsider riding out alone. It just might not be safe like it was when we were kids."

Kat heard the change in his tone, the simmering undercurrent of a thinly disguised threat. She wheeled Blue around. Her recalcitrant nature that had led her to punch him when she was a girl exploded through her veneer of calm. She refused to be threatened by this bully. Despite what he said to the contrary, she was confident that he'd not changed his stripes.

As only a woman can, she channeled the rage, smiling sweetly. "Thank you for the warning, Liam. It's nice to know you're concerned." She reached down and patted the butt of her rifle tucked into the leather scabbard. "I'll be sure to keep my Browning fully loaded."

Turning Blue's head for home, she kneed the mare into a run, smiling as she leaned forward into the wind.

Nightmares and Premonitions

IMMERSED IN A freezing fog of snow that stung his ears and fingers, Jonathan strained to make out the indistinct trail ahead. The world was a colorless white, a silent blanket muffling the sound of his horse's hooves. The absence of sound accentuated the horse's labored breathing as she struggled through knee-deep drifts. His own ragged breath struggled to keep pace with his pounding heart. He was racing time itself, a cruel enemy that nipped at his horse's heels like a wolf in winter. Each step seemed to take an agonizing lifetime, a precious lifetime, *her* precious lifetime. Pulling at his horse's hooves, time conspired against them.

Cold grabbed at his fingers, sending needles of pain up into his arm. Although every extremity was numb, stung by the frigid winds, sweat ran in rivulets down his chest.

The world changed again, no longer white, but red. Crimson like the sun setting behind a prairie fire, scorching the sky and land. Heat, not cold, spread flames across his chest and down his arms. His flesh seemed to melt with its intensity, the fabric of his shirt sticking to his skin. He cast his eyes down to his arm, where sweat stained his shirt crimson, like blood. As if his heart were demanding its freedom from the constraints of his chest, his pulse beat wildly in his ears, loud and insistent.

Blond mane flew up into his face, acting like a fan, relieving the burning of his skin. *But Jessie is a bay. Yes, a bay with black mane and tail.* The blond mane brushed silky soft against his face, smelling faintly of lavender. *How odd.*

The girl's head lolled to the side and fell heavily against his shoulder. He glanced down at the white bodice of her dress, stained red. His hand, holding her tight to his body, keeping her from falling, was crimson as well. Red streaks slid down his horse's leg and drops stained the snow.

In the next moment the body of the girl had slipped from his arms crumpling to the ground, enfolded by a quilt of snow. She looked as though asleep, her hair arrayed about her head like a golden halo, her skin pale as winter's moon. She was a star that had fallen, confused for a delicate flake of snow cast down to the earth.

And then he was kneeling in the snow at her side, lifting her head ever so gently so as not to disturb her slumber. Cradling her head in the crook of his arm, he brushed the fine strands of pale hair from her ashen cheek, feather soft, her icy skin biting his fingertips. With his hand lightly resting on the cords of her neck, he could feel her pulse accelerate for one moment before it ceased. Three slow beats tapped against his finger until at last the bird within broke free of its fleshly prison.

Once more the colors merged and transformed. Silky soft against his arm, her hair appeared no longer as pale strands of blond, but brown. Chestnut colored curls framed her face. As he reached to touch them, they fell away from her face and her lifeless eyes looked up unseeing, not blue but brown.

The fog that was the dream lifted like a curtain. With a sickening awareness, he saw that the girl in his arms was not the girl who had haunted his dreams this past year, but was instead, Kat Meriwether. Those steaming pools of blood swelled and grew, fed by her gaping wound.

He yelled out, "No!" The dream clung to him as he slogged back to reality, refusing to be shaken off.

"Jonathan, wake up." The voice came as though from a body buried deep within the snow. "Jonathan. It's all right." The voice was more insistent this time. The dream fought to keep him, but the voice would not be silenced.

"Jonathan, it's all right."

But it wasn't all right. She was dead. He had failed to save her. Nothing was *all* right. He was not *all* right.

With a suddenness that made his head swim, Jonathan sat up. His hands flew to his face. Pushing his fingertips into a steeple, his thumbs pressing the bridge of his nose, he rocked forward, eyes straining to focus. This was real, the rough wood planks beneath his feet, the musty smell of his blanket, daylight streaming through the dirty window. This was reality, not the dream.

"Jonathan?" The voice attached itself to a face. Timothy sat at the foot of the bunk, his face pinched in concern. Adam stood in the doorway, his eyes wide with fear.

Jonathan ran trembling fingers through his hair. His attempt to smile came as little more than a pained thin line. "It was just a bad dream."

"Adam, go bring us a cup of coffee." Timothy shot Adam a stern look when the boy hesitated in the doorway.

The boy ran, his feet hammering a worried rhythm back to the main house.

Jonathan stood up and shuffled to the wash stand where he picked up the pitcher, pouring cold water into the bowl. After splashing a handful on his face and the back of his neck, he grabbed a towel, holding it over his face for long moments until his pulse slowed.

Timothy watched him, his hands rubbing the knees of his pants in long slow strokes. "The boy came to see what was keeping you from coming to breakfast this morning." The big man stood and shoved his hands into his pockets, as though hiding his hands might help to hide his discomfort. "You were...talking in your sleep. He was scared when he couldn't wake you, so he came to get me." His explanation seemed an attempt to excuse his intrusion on Jonathan's private agony.

"Sorry to have given him a scare," Jonathan said flatly. He reached for the razor and saw his hand shaking. Turning back to face Timothy, he managed a wry smile. "It was just a nightmare, probably something I ate. No offense to your cooking."

"I know it's not my place to meddle in a man's affairs, but it isn't just a bad dream is it? When we were driving those cattle north, the boy and I heard you cry out in your sleep many times. What happened back in Texas?"

Jonathan turned to the window, eyes focused on the paddock where he could see Jessie pacing, tossing her head, impatient for breakfast. This was something that needed to stay buried, and if it came out at night to haunt his dreams then that's where it must stay. He'd have to live with it just like he lived with his failure as one sworn to protect the innocent.

Jonathan sighed heavily. And yet, maybe he did need to trust someone. Timothy deserved some explanation. Without turning, he said softly, "I made a mistake, an error in judgment, and my mistake cost a young girl her life."

"Is that why you quit the Rangers?"

"Yes." Jonathan propped the hand mirror on the window sill. He picked up the razor again and studied his reflection. Behind him, he could see Timothy staring at his back, his face awash with questions and pity, neither of which Jonathan wanted.

Timothy stood, walking slowly to the door. He turned at the doorframe. Jonathan still held the razor tenuously against his chin.

"It's a heavy burden you're carrying on only two shoulders. I think of you as a friend, Jonathan. I'd like to help if I can." He turned without waiting for Jonathan to reply and walked from the cabin.

Jonathan stared at his reflection for a moment, putting down his razor again. Leaning on the table, he peered into the water, calm within the basin. The dream was bad enough, to come night after night. But why had it changed? Why had *her* face become Kat Meriwether's face? He didn't want to think about the possible explanations. He didn't want to think about any of it! He wasn't a superstitious man, one given to premonitions or signs. But his confidence in his abilities as a lawman had been shaken because he'd underestimated the capacity of evil in one man. He hadn't seen the signs then. He didn't want to miss them now. So, if there were signs, even in his dreams, he needed to understand them.

Taking on textures and scents, the metallic smell of blood, the dream seemed even more real this time. His fingers held the memory of the soft hair at the nape of her neck, and the smell of lavender seemed even now to fill the room. The chestnut curls were those of the attractive young doctor. He closed his eyes, but the memory and the fragrance of her would not leave him.

"But Father, we've not stayed this long in one place before. Doesn't it make sense to pull up stakes now, before someone figures out what we're up to?" Ethan couldn't sit still any longer listening to his father discuss their next job with outrageous calm. He paced to the window and back again.

"Ethan, it's all under control." Hall sat back in his chair and pulled at the cigar clenched in his teeth. "You're worrying about a gnat. Doc Meriwether hasn't said anything and I doubt he will. And as far as that girl of his, well, all I need for you to do is apply a bit of that school-boy charm."

"But this isn't our style. We've always hit the fields where the strikes are new and the mines haven't been taken over by the big businesses. We've been in and out before they've organized. We're taking too many chances now. I've heard that the miners have hired more guards for the wagon runs." Ethan sensed he was talking to a wall, that his father had turned a deaf ear. This was different as well. Before coming here, he'd always managed to cajole his father into his way of thinking.

He glanced over to where a man sat in the shadowed corner of the room, the new man his father had bragged to Kat Meriwether would bring an end to the robberies. Ethan had experienced a growing sense of uneasiness from the first moment of their meeting, this man known only to him as Cahill.

He tried again. "Look, there's a new strike north, off the Snake River. I've heard they're pulling out a lot of color. The news is spreading and that means more mines and more ore to be packed out. Let's light out and get ourselves set up early."

Gilford Hall shook his head slowly, blowing a lazy curl of smoke from his fat lips. "That all sounds fine, but the fact is, I'm comfortable here." He squeezed his eyes shut and sucked his teeth before saying, "We've got a real sweet thing going here. I've earned some respect. I've got a fine house. I'd be a fool to give this up."

"You can do the same thing over towards Silver City. Let me take some of the men over to the new strike on the east side of the Sawtooth Range. We'll hit now before they can get organized, just like we've always done." Ethan despised himself for the pleading tone in his voice. But he couldn't shake the growing sense that their long string of luck was about to run out. It was time to fold. As surely as he knew it, he knew his father would not be persuaded to see the wisdom of moving on.

The man in the corner chuckled. "Seems your boy's backbone is turning to mush."

Ethan whirled on him, shooting him a narrowed-eyed challenge. "I've got plenty of grit, Cahill! What are you bringing to this?"

The man bored a hole through Ethan with dangerous eyes, his voice, deep and menacing. He patted the gleaming Colt strapped to his hip. "I got this."

Ethan felt his hackles rise. This was just the kind of powder keg of a man that would get them all hanged. He knew it as sure as he knew his father would not be persuaded to leave Snowberry. His father seemed deaf and dumb to the town rumblings growing against him. Either his arrogance or his ignorance had blinded him to the danger Ethan saw daily building around them.

Someone would connect the dots soon enough. When they did, he wanted to be long gone, as far from Snowberry as he could get, maybe even out of the territory. The irony was that the petite and beguiling Dr. Meriwether might be the one to fit those pieces together first. He didn't want to be around when she did. More to the point of it, he didn't want to be the one to stop her. But his father didn't need him for that anymore. He had Cahill.

Chapter 15

Pleasant Distractions

ON THE MORNING of the picnic Kat woke early to attend to her dubious duties as chairman of the food contests. The irony of that appointment was not wasted on her father, who laughed loud and long when he'd heard of it.

Before leaving the house, she checked herself in the mirror once more. One petticoat seemed quite enough for such an event, considering the small bustle she argued herself into wearing. Her figure showed off to greatest advantage by the fitted bodice of her blue silk dress. The waistline dipped to a narrow "v". It was a dress that would have been severe except for the touch of deeper blue velvet at the throat and matching velvet bows at the top of the four tailored skirt pleats. An insert of ivory lace behind each pleat made the gathered skirt appear even fuller than it was, further softening the overall effect. But Kat was particularly pleased with the slight ruching of the sleeves, just the thing to add a feminine touch to a practical tailored dress. She nodded with satisfaction to her reflection, then turned to the door where her father stood watching her.

"You don't think I'm overdressed for a picnic, do you?" She touched the back of her hair, testing the stability of the pins holding her curls in place atop her head. As usual the thickness of her hair rebelled at the forced restriction, gravity tugging at strands from the coiled coiffure.

"Little girl, don't you dare change a thing. You're perfect."

Skipping the three steps that separated them, Kat looped her arm through his. "Thank you so much for agreeing to be a judge again this year."

"Well, I've never turned down an offer of free food," he said. He opened the door and made a slight bow. "Shall we?"

Pressed on three sides by red-faced women, Kat was surrounded with no avenue of escape.

Pushing angrily at a strand of hair that had shaken loose from her upswept hair, Mrs. Townsend leaned in, inches from Kat's ear. "Well, I think it's definitely not a legal entry! Apple strudel is simply not a pie!"

Kat threw Mrs. Forester a pleading look. Mrs. Forester smiled benevolently, but stood stoically to the side, well out of range.

No help there, she thought. What had she gotten into! This would require some diplomacy and a large dose of patience. She stared blankly at the two women waiting for her to respond. The buttons of their bodices seemed threatened by the heaving of their chests. Mrs. Victoria Townsend's face was flushed with apoplectic rage. Perhaps she'd need to administer a bit of digitalis for heart strain before this went too far. She relaxed a bit as the humor of their accusations of contest violation struck her.

"Dr. Meriwether, I hardly think this is cause for mirth." Mrs. Hermione Schuster's eyes narrowed to slits.

Kat hadn't realized that her face had betrayed her, allowing a smile to escape. She drew the corners of her mouth down, then cast her eyes to the offending strudel. "No, I suppose it isn't."

"Certainly not! So, what do you propose to do about this?" Mrs. Victoria Townsend threw back.

The 'pie' in question was undoubtedly the most visually appealing entry on the table. She looked at the number on the tag, then checked her entry list. That was interesting. Timothy Hindricks. That was the man she'd treated for the argument with the mule. She smiled at the memory of his embarrassment.

Hearing Mrs. Townsend make a distinct 'harrumph', she realized that the smile had tugged the corners of her mouth upward again. An instant later she successfully managed to lower her brow into a proper scowl.

Kat needed to take control. It was expected. So she cleared her throat and announced, "Well, it certainly doesn't fit into the cake category, or even the cookie category."

She paused, her mind racing ahead to resolve the issue with as little bloodletting as possible. As much as she recognized the inequality of the treatment of women in this the cusp of the twentieth century, she was honest enough to realize that justice must work in two directions. If women excelled in cooking, but a man was willing to challenge that superiority, who was she to stand in the way.

She took in a long inhalation of tense air. "It may not be a *conventional* pie but I really can't see that we can reject the entry for any sound reason. Our..." She paused here assessing her audience. "Our biases should not limit the competition."

There was a sharp intake of breath from both Mrs. Victoria Townsend and Mrs. Hermione Schuster.

Kat pulled herself to her full five feet two inches. Knowing her boots had added an inch to that, she charged ahead before either woman could give voice to their objections. "So, with the authority vested in me by this committee, I will accept the entry. We'll let the judges decide, and may the best man or woman win!"

The two storm clouds rained down on each other as Kat excused herself, rapidly walking away to a sunnier location, but not before Mrs. Hermione Schuster had commented quite loudly, "Next I suppose men will be allowed to enter the needlework competitions!"

Kat recalled with amusement that her dress had been designed by a man, but she held her tongue on that matter. *Never again*, she thought.

"Ah, come on, Mr. Winthrop, it'll be fun!"

Jonathan straightened, the pitchfork providing a support for his arm as he gave Adam a bemused expression that spread from his eyes to his lips. "Fun?"

"Yeah. There'll be games and lots of food." Adam's face screwed up as he thought of ways to entice Jonathan to join them. He tried another tack. "And I'm betting that pretty lady doctor will be there too!"

"You planning on asking her to dance, are 'ya?" Jonathan asked.

Adam scratched the back of his leg with his big toe. "Aw, she won't pay any attention to me." Then his face brightened. He added, "But she might with you."

A vision of the Dr. Meriwether out of his dream swam to the forefront of his mind, the smell of lavender and the cascading curls the color of chestnut, the softness of the skin at the nape of her neck. As quickly as the memory came warming his blood, the second part of the dream replaced the warmth with a chilling cold. He'd seen those lifeless brown eyes, her eyes staring out of an ashen face.

He shook his head as if to dislodge the dream, thrusting the pitchfork deep into the hay. "Best, you and your dad go along without me." His mouth turned into a grim line.

Adam kicked at the dirt and turned to go, hands shoved into his pockets. He appeared to remember something and turned back. "Father told me there was another attempted robbery of another ore wagon, but no one got hurt this time. Guess the miners have bought themselves some hired guns." When Jonathan didn't respond to the news, Adam shuffled back to the house.

Although Jonathan took in the news without comment, he'd heard it well enough. He propped the pitchfork against the barn wall then walked to the paddock. Resting his arms on the top rail, he gazed out on the distant hills, layers in hazy shades of blue stretching as far as the eye could see. Although the sky was clear, his mind's eye envisioned the storm descending on this peaceful river valley. He felt it as surely as he felt the sun's warmth on his back. Drawing a hand across his face, he felt suddenly very old. What made him think it would be any different here?

The violence would escalate now. Innocents would be caught in the crossfire. New markers would be made for the town cemetery. Good men would try to stop what was coming, and die. But this wasn't his war. This wasn't his responsibility to stop them. No star on his chest called him to duty.

But the girl with the chestnut hair could become one of the innocents to be caught in the crossfire sure to come. If the dream had come as an omen, was it his warning? Was she his responsibility to protect? One more question stirred. Might he be given a second chance to redeem himself?

If he became involved, it had to be about protecting Kat Meriwether and nothing more. There was no room in his life for such a woman, she so full of possibilities and he with so few. She had her youth and a promising future. He had grown weary of the ugliness in the world, losing hope that one man could do much to restrain it. The evil he'd seen had eclipsed his youth, leaving him feeling old and used up.

Adam had his foot on the wagon's running board when he heard his father call out. "Didn't think you were interested in coming with us."

The boy turned to see Jonathan striding across the yard leading Jessie. Adam had never seen him like this, dressed in dark pants and shirt, clothes that fit like he'd been grown in them. His hair showed wet where it stuck out from beneath his hat, as if he'd just washed it. Even his boots looked as though he'd taken the time to do more than just brush the dust off. They actually had a shine. But the difference that drew the boy's attention first and last was the gun now strapped to the man's hip. Hanging low and strapped down, it would be an easy reach for his right hand. It looked as natural there as dust on a hat.

Adam's mouth hung open, gaping at the suddenly transformed cowpuncher. Jonathan walked up to him and poked his chin with his finger. "Better close that before the flies make a home." Jonathan pushed Adam up into the wagon then grabbed the saddle horn, mounting Jessie in one seemingly effortless movement.

Seeing their surprised faces, he thought to give an explanation for his change of mind, so he volunteered, "Well, I guess I need to see for myself if the fine citizens of Snowberry appreciate your good cookin' as much as Adam and I do. If there's any justice left in Idaho, you should be coming home with a blue ribbon."

Timothy snorted. "Glad you changed your mind." He slapped the reins against the mules' rumps, calling out, "Gee'up!"

Chapter 16

Veiled and Unveiled

BEHIND THE CHURCH, rough sawn planks stretched out on sawhorses in long rows under the shade provided by ancient cedar trees. The women of Snowberry had brought out their everyday linens to cover the coarse wood lumber, while the children had gathered wildflowers, sticking them into jars of water placed randomly down their lengths. Dappled shade made lacelike patterns over all, creating an overall effect that Kat found delightful. In her opinion, no elegant crystal dining experience in all of Boston compared to the beauty of this charming provincial setting.

For days the Ladies Missionary Aide Society had busied themselves preparing their best casseroles and bakery items to tempt Snowberry's residents. Sagging under the weight of all those dishes, the serving table groaned, scarcely able to accommodate them all. On a separate table, plates full of cookies and tins of golden crusted pies competed with two-layer cakes and temptingly fragrant cinnamon rolls.

Kat finished placing ribbons on the winning entries of baked goods. Although it would precipitate an extensive and very specific rewriting of the rules for entries in next year's confections' contest, she was secretly delighted that Mr. Hindricks' apple strudel had won top honor. Besides, it would give the ladies of Snowberry twelve months to improve on his recipe for next year. When she had placed the ribbon on his greatly contested strudel, she found it nearly impossible to suppress an impish smile.

Appraising each delectable dish with care, Nathaniel Meriwether strolled down the length of the table offering baked goods for sale. Infamous for his sweet tooth, the ladies of Snowberry's Missionary Aide Society watched him with keen interest. No small degree of pride would flood the heart of she whose confection he selected. Besides, he was still a very attractive man, and many a widow had set her sights on him over the years. Perhaps one might not only win the ribbon but the greater prize of the doctor himself. Such motivation had spurred many inspirational confections.

"Papa!" Kat saw him from across the grass covered lawn, hailing him with her voice and waving hand. She had to weave her way around the cheering children waiting in line for the next sack race. The volume of their cheers indicated the closeness of the match currently in progress. Josie's brother, Jeremy, tugged her sleeve as she walked through the line of children. "Dr. Meriwether, won't you please be my partner?"

Kat pulled up looking down into the boy's glum expression. "Can't you find a partner, Jeremy?"

"Nah. Billy says it's kid's stuff. He didn't think so last year and we won three races!"

Kat glanced down at her long skirt regretting her choice in attire. Had she chosen to wear her split skirt, perhaps she could have joined him and maintained a degree of propriety in the eyes of the ladies of Snowberry. But as she was currently dressed, she might cause a scandal of historic proportions if she indulged her whim of joining him. Still, she was sorely tempted.

Her eyes cast about the growing crowd of picnickers and onlookers for someone who might help her young friend. A man in a tan Stetson with a wide brim shielding his face stood out from the crowd. In the next moment she recognized him as Jonathan Winthrop, and next to him stood his young friend, Adam. Grabbing Jeremy by the hand, she deftly wove a path through the children to the two.

"Good day! Jonathan. Adam." She was a bit breathless when she spoke, the irritating result of wearing a corset. *Accursed thing*, she thought as she straightened her posture to allow air back into her diaphragm.

Jonathan tipped his hat. "Ma'am."

Adam's face split open in a grin at the sight of her. "Hello, Dr. Meriwether."

"I'm so glad you're here. This is my friend, Jeremy, and he is in dire need of a partner for the three-legged race. He's quite a runner I hear. I was wondering if it isn't too much to ask if you would be his partner?"

Adam hadn't taken his eyes off Kat. True those eyes had slipped a bit from her face to take in her shapely figure, but he was fully attending to her. As she awaited his reply, he continued to gaze at her with his mouth slightly ajar.

Jonathan nudged Adam with his elbow. "Adam! The lady asked you a question. You going to answer?"

Adam glanced up at Jonathan. "Huh?"

"She asked if you would run in a race with Jeremy," Jonathan explained.

Adam turned back to Kat and then looked at the boy standing to her side. "Oh! Run a race! Sure." The truth be told, he'd have performed cartwheels across the yard if she'd asked it of him.

"Well then. . .Jeremy, go take your new partner and give those other kids a run for their money!" Kat tousled Jeremy's hair and shooed them both away with a wave of her hand.

When the two boys had run off to join the line waiting their turn to race, Jonathan said, "That was kind of you, Dr. Meriwether. Adam doesn't know many boys his age."

Her hand shielding her face from the midday sun, Kat turned back to face him. "Oh, well, I'm sure it wasn't a purely selfless motive on my part." She took hold of the side of her dress and pulled it wide, laughing lightly. "He asked me to race with him. I'm sure I would've created a scandal had I raced across the field with my petticoat showing."

Jonathan nodded solemnly. "Yes, ma'am, I surely suppose that it would."

Oh my, when did I become so bold as to speak of petticoats with someone I barely know? But he was so easy to talk with. Changing the subject, she asked, "Did Mr. Hindricks come to the picnic as well? I've been meaning to pay him a visit. How's his. . .injury?"

"Oh, he's mending. Stands a lot more these days." He gave her a knowing look.

She laughed lightly, realizing that it might not be the most professional reaction. "Yes, I would suppose he would." An awkward pause followed, leaving Kat to wonder what her hands were doing as they seemed to independently flutter about her hair, testing pins and toying with stray strands. *Good Lord!* She felt like a school girl in his presence.

"Looks like the boys are up next." Jonathan pointed to the front of the line of boys and girls crowding to the starting line. With a sudden swelling of children's voices, the runners set off for a ribbon strung between two trees at the end of the field. Jonathan leaned close to her ear to be heard above the noise of the screaming children. "Looks like they got this one."

She experienced a sudden tingling down her back as his warm breath touched her neck, a pleasant sensation not unlike having a feather brush against her skin. Giving him a faint smile, she found her throat strangely constricted. A light remark would have been appropriate, but words oddly failed her.

"My brother and I used to beat the britches off anyone when we were youngsters. Gatherings like these weren't too common in our part of Texas. But when we did have a chance to run, no one could stop us." Jonathan's eyes were on the cheering crowd, his voice having taken on the quality of a warm memory.

"Was he older or younger than you?" Kat felt relief to have found her mind engaging her voice again.

"Older."

Kat heard the shift in tone to one no longer filled with the warmth of fond memories.

As if assessing her for something, Jonathan turned his head, looking down at her for a moment. He said, "He was killed in the war."

"Oh." Kat heard the weight of the simple statement. "I'm so sorry." She felt somewhat disquieted by the intensity of his gaze. Was he expecting her to say more? At last he spoke, his slow Texas drawl measuring his words, "Most of us are. . .sorry that is, about the war. Lot of good men died."

"Yes." She saw in his serious face more than the words would reveal. Those dark, brooding eyes had seen too much suffering. She'd seen the look in doctors who'd served on both sides of the war. In her years training in the hospital, she'd watched patients die and experience unbearable pain, but her personal experience was limited. This man had known such suffering.

Cheering voices drew their attention back to the race as Jeremy and Adam streaked across the finish line in the second race.

"Seems they're a winning pair," he said.

Kat clapped her hands and waved to Jeremy whose face was alight with victory.

"That boy doesn't seem to let his lack of height hold him back, does he?" Jonathan smiled at her and for a moment his eyes seemed bluer than gray as though the true color, as with his true nature, were unveiled for just one candid moment.

"He seems to take after his mother." She laughed. "She and I used to...how did you put it? We used to beat the britches off everyone."

Jonathan threw her a skeptical look. "You? With those short legs of yours?"

"I'll have you know, we won all the sack races and the three-legged races for three years in a row! Josie and I were unbeatable!" She folded her arms across her waist. "It's not nearly as much about the legs as it is about the heart!"

He met her eyes with one eyebrow lifted a degree higher than the other before the corners of his mouth tugged upward into a smile. "Well now, I suspect that might be true. That would mean that you've got one very big heart."

As much as she'd initially disliked the idea of the picnic, she'd couldn't think of anything she'd rather do than sit all afternoon with this gentle giant of a man, talking with him about anything and nothing. It was a funny thought that fired messages from one lobe of her brain to the other. He made her feel incredibly at ease in his presence at the same time as making her feel dreadfully uncomfortable. She brought her hand quickly to her ear, giving it a good pinch.

A waving hand from across the yard caught her eye. Kat motioned to her father to join them. "Papa! Come meet one of our newest Snowberry residents."

Nathaniel Meriwether extended his hand first and Jonathan took it firmly in his. In that moment of meeting, Kat could see the steady assessment, each man of the other. She knew her father to be a man of keen observation and she rather thought that Jonathan Winthrop might be such a man himself, both in a long moment taking a mental measurement of the other.

"Mr. Winthrop and his friend Mr. Hindricks are working cattle on the Schmidt's Valley homestead. Remember, when I asked you about who had moved in?"

"Oh, yes! That's a beautiful place. My daughter and I used to take rides up there, fishing the south end of the river that runs through it. Have you discovered that sweet little fishing hole yet?"

"Not yet. We've been pretty busy just making the place livable. Haven't had much opportunity to take time off. This is the first day we've really taken any time away except to pick up necessary things at the mercantile."

"That's not surprising." Nathaniel cast a longing look back at the tables of food. "I hope you came with an appetite, Mr. Winthrop. We've got some of the best cooks in all Idaho Territory right here. Since it's all for a good cause, would you let me buy you some of their best? I will advise you on what will make you think you've entered a gastronomical paradise. More importantly, I can steer you clear of those that might have you spending a very long night in the privy." He leaned forward and whispered, "That would be Mrs. Kimball's pork pie. She insists that marinating the meat for two days on her kitchen counter is the secret. It most undoubtedly is the secret that's made many a resident pay me a visit the day after the picnic, complaining of intense abdominal pain."

Jonathan's serious face broke for a moment, just short of allowing a smile to soften his expression.

"Father, that sounds like an excellent idea. Why don't you and Mr. Winthrop be the first in line? I've got some things to do at the judge's table." It was a lie, but her proximity to Jonathan Winthrop was making it difficult to think of anything other than...well...things. These were the things that she'd resolved would distract her from her short-range goal as well as her long-range ones, and Mr. Winthrop was definitely becoming a hazard.

Turning abruptly, she lifted the hem of her skirt and walked swiftly away, leaving them standing somewhat perplexed at her sudden departure. Could she have managed to run in her close-fitting petticoat, she might have beaten the youngsters racing across the field to the finish line.

Nathaniel and Jonathan strolled to the serving line, selecting a wide assortment of dishes to share. It was obvious that Jonathan had a weakness for fried chicken, since he selected three different dishes. Nathaniel had an inclination toward anything beef, the more gravy the better. Both agreed to wait on the desserts.

Between bites, Nathaniel provided Jonathan with an historical survey of the long valley that stretched north to the Snake River. He told of the Bannock and Paiutes Indians' influence on development, the recent growth of ranching that was developing to supply the mining camps. In the brief history of Idaho Territory, there had been many skirmishes between Indians, shepherds and cattlemen, miners and ranchers. In short, everyone fought everyone. The recent war was not the only scar upon the land. Nathaniel observed that violence seemed to spread outward from the eastern shores, fueled by greed.

"Your accent tells me you've spent a good deal of time in Texas. That's a territory that has certainly known its share of bloody conflict," Nathaniel said matter-of-factly, an open invitation for Jonathan to contribute a bit of his own history.

Jonathan just nodded. "Yes, sir, it has indeed." He didn't elaborate.

There was a stirring of voices behind Nathaniel, prompting both men to look in the direction of the commotion. Nathaniel turned back to his meal, his face suddenly losing its good-natured expression. Jonathan noted the change.

"Doc! Haven't seen you in church lately, not since that girl of yours come home." Gilford Hall threw a heavy hand on Nathaniel's shoulder. Nathaniel closed his eyes, taking a heavy breath.

"That's true." It was flat, thin.

Another man stood a few paces back from Hall, his expression making no attempt to adapt to the festive occasion. Jonathan studied him with professional interest, the width of his shoulders that spoke of strength, the constant movement of his eyes left and right as he scanned the crowd. There was a tension in his body that suggested a loaded spring. The manner in which he wore his gun, not too low, but within easy reach, with the hammer filed, bespoke his true profession.

At last, the man brought his eyes to rest on Jonathan. In a moment they had changed to steel, assessing the threat of him. The man's brow furrowed for just a moment, the spring tightening.

Gilford Hall threw his leg over the bench, sitting close to Nathaniel. He reached to Nathaniel's plate and picked up a piece of ham. After stuffing it in his mouth, he licked his fingers, grinning. "Oh my! That must be Mrs. Townsend's smoked ham." He turned his head sharply to take in Jonathan across the table.

"Don't think we've met. Name's Gilford Hall."

"Jonathan. Jonathan Winthrop."

"Oh, you're Hindricks' hired hand." There was something dismissive in the way he stressed the word *hired*.

Jonathan picked up another leg of chicken, tearing off a piece with his teeth.

"Somebody told me you were from Texas. That right?" Hall reached across the table toward Jonathan's plate. Jonathan stabbed his fork into the leg of chicken that Hall had started for. The fork came down hard, within a hair's breadth of the man's hand.

Hall jerked his hand back, eyes wide.

Jonathan lifted the fork with the chicken leg attached, sniffed it and slowly handed it to the man.

Hall gave a snort and took the fork from Jonathan. He pulled the leg from the fork and returned the fork to Jonathan. Pulling a piece of meat from the bone, he chewed slowly, his eyes never leaving Jonathan's face. After a long moment he put the half-eaten leg on Nathaniel's plate.

"Never cared much for Mrs. Anderson's chicken, way overcooked." He wiped his mouth with the back of his hand. With forced casualness, he rose to his feet. Slapping Nathaniel's shoulder again, he said, "Good to see you, Doc. Glad you're here to take care of our good citizens. Would be a shame to lose you, or your girl. People have come to depend on you."

He threw a half-smile at Jonathan along with a cold stare, sharply contradicting his friendly speech. "Real nice to meet you, Mr. Winthrop. Hope I can get to know you better."

The man with the gun remained, his eyes riveted on Jonathan. In his expression was an unmistakable challenge. Jonathan nodded to him. The man backed away without saying a word. Turning slowly, he followed Hall.

Nathaniel let out a ragged breath, staring at Jonathan as if seeing him for the first time. At last he spoke. "Did you know that man?"

"Don't think so. But I know his type." Jonathan stabbed a slice of beef.

"I've got to admit, that I've heard the rumors, Jonathan. Are you a lawman like they say?"

Jonathan pushed his plate to the side. With slow movements he placed his hands on the table in front of him, staring at them for long moments before looking up to meet Nathaniel's curious gaze. His Texas drawl seemed more pronounced as he answered, drawing out the first word.

"Well, I don't know what the rumors are sayin', but I can tell you straight that I was a Texas Ranger." His gray eyes appeared to grow darker, "I *was*, but not anymore." He sat back and looked beyond Nathaniel to follow the passage of the two men as they worked their way through the crowd of townspeople. "I decided it was time to move into another line of work," he said.

Nathaniel heard the weight of the word, the unspoken history of it. "But you're a young man yet."

"Age had nothing to do with it."

"Ah." It was all Nathaniel said in reply. He studied his plate, pushing the remnants of his meal into neat piles.

Jonathan watched him, a tightness forming around his mouth. "But I need to ask you, Dr. Meriwether, if you understood that Hall just threatened both you and your daughter?"

Nathaniel lifted his eyes slowly to meet Jonathan's. He sighed heavily. "Afraid I did, yes."

"You know something. You saw something."

The silence grew heavy and telling. This was all too familiar, something he'd witnessed before, that reluctance to trust, the crippling fear. Jonathan assessed that the man was not a coward. He also surmised that had his daughter not been privy to this bit of evidence, the doctor would have spoken of it. But what was it he knew, and did it really implicate the sheriff? Why else would he threaten him?

The turmoil that roiled in his gut, was how much should he encourage the man to speak what he knew. The last time he'd done that. . .He felt the cold sweat of his nightmares.

Across the grassy field a fiddle sang out a cheerful reel. A dozen young men and women danced under the cool shade of the cedars, their merry voices mingling with the tune. Jonathan caught sight of Kat's blue dress and chestnut curls, a handsome man close at her side. He noted the manner in which the young man held her elbow leaning in close to speak to her. It was the man he'd seen earlier cleaning her shoes outside the mercantile.

"Dr. Meriwether, who is that man with your daughter?" Jonathan asked.

Nathaniel's forehead creased, "That's Ethan Hall, the sheriff's boy."

Those familiar alarms rang ominously inside Jonathan's head. He frowned watching the familiarity of the man with Nathaniel's daughter. What better way to find out what the two doctors suspected than to win her confidence? She laughed at something Hall had said. Jonathan chewed on his lower lip, considering what he might do to interfere with the man's attempts to cajole information out of her.

If they were involved in the wagon attacks and the murder, Jonathan was certain that they'd find a way to cover the evidence, stopping at nothing to protect themselves. A slow awareness of pain caused him to look down at his hand where blood dripped from the palm onto the grass beneath the rough bench. He released his grip on the bench to see a splinter of wood protruding from the skin. He stared down at it for a moment before extracting it, absently wiping the blood away.

A Ranger's Sense

THE CONTENTS OF two plates of cookies showered down about Kat like fall leaves as her shocked face once more met that of Ethan Hall. She closed her eyes, then quickly knelt to retrieve the scattered confections.

"We meet again, Mr. Hall," she said through tight lips.

Ethan knelt beside her, pulling a smashed butter cookie from beneath his knee. "Yes indeed, Dr. Meriwether. We seem to have some destiny working for us." He threw her a charming grin of amusement.

As she retrieved two chocolate cookies from beneath the table, Kat entertained the thought that perhaps destiny was working against her rather than the other way around. When they'd both collected all they could, Kat held a rather sad assortment of cookies in various stages of crumble, mixed in with a generous portion of organic matter.

"Guess I'll just buy both of these. It's for a good cause after all." Ethan took one of the plates, leaving Kat to follow with the second.

Waiting for him to make his purchase, she watched as he stuffed his jacket pockets with the broken pieces. She couldn't help but laugh, conceding to herself that it was a generous manner of apology.

After hearing her laugh, Ethan looked down at himself, his pockets bulging. He tipped his head to the side, shrugging his shoulders. Popping one broken piece in his mouth he offered her another, which she accepted.

Ethan was an easy conversationalist, a carefully honed skill. He saw it as a professional necessity which had served him well. Out of the most taciturn gentlemen, Ethan could draw information he might not otherwise wish to share. Over an amiable game of cards perhaps, or sharing a drink, he gleaned an amazing amount of valuable secrets which could be exchanged for a lucrative profit. He was talented at being an insightful companion and a sympathetic listener. Both men and women found themselves drawing him into their confidences by what they determined to be his personal interest in them. With the men he was a perfect companion, one who could tell a bawdy joke very well and drink to apparent excess. With the women, he could use his pale blue eyes like a snake charmer, mesmerizing them into trusting him. With his soft voice and gentleman's courtesies, he rarely had to overwhelm or strong-arm his way into anyone's secrets, rather, he was invited in for tea and confessions.

However, Kat presented a challenge to him. When he thought he was squeezing through that sturdy door of her polite exterior, she could skillfully slam it shut. Like Jonathan, he had a talent for assessing people. This woman was smart and she was driven. He could see her leading some women's suffrage parade, a sash of protest tied neatly at her very trim waist. He hadn't had much experience with such women, but he believed that beneath the veneer of self-sufficiency there was a very needy young woman. Of course, he would be the very thing she needed, or so he would convince her. How unfortunate that he actually liked her.

"It seems as if you may be staying with us awhile. That's wonderful." It wasn't difficult for him to sound sincere. In contrast to the town's offerings, her company would be a welcome change.

"I'll help as long as I feel my father needs me."

Ethan considered that fact and filed it away. He ventured an observation, "It seems that could be a sacrifice for someone of your education and professional goals. Even Boise has more to offer a physician than our humble town. What with the new capital, train depot up on the bench above town, new hotels, I'd think a young woman would be eager to be a part of such a thriving community." It was flattery on Ethan's part, but he was also curious to learn why such an attractive and talented woman would return to this provincial setting. He genuinely wanted to hear her answer.

Kat allowed herself to be escorted across the grounds. "I would think that I might ask the same of you."

Ethan's step hesitated. "Care to elaborate?"

"Well, you seem to be a man of some education, and I would think there were few opportunities here for you as well. You don't seem to have an interest in either farming or ranching. Is there a business you are interested in pursuing here?"

This was unexpected. It shouldn't have been. In a few steps, she had turned the tables on him, prying him for information. It was a dangerous tack for her to take.

"That's a very good question." He recovered his smile. "You are correct in assuming I have some education. My father saw to that." He continued, "He hopes to turn me into a banker. With the town growing and more ranchers moving into the valley, he's hoping to establish a formalized banking institution. These people deserve something more than biscuit tins under their beds." This was a hastily constructed lie, but one he'd employed before. There was a degree of truth in it, he supposed. The bank would simply be one of deposit with no withdrawals.

"I see."

Something in her voice, a faint but unmistakable shimmer of doubt, made him wonder at just how much she knew. "Do you dance, Dr. Meriwether?" He inclined his head.

Kat granted him a genuine smile. "Indeed, Mr. Hall, I do."

He took her hand in his while slipping his other hand to her waist. The music drew them into the swirling, laughing ring of dancers. The lone fiddler had been joined by two others, another with a banjo. For a time, neither Kat nor Ethan attempted to take from the other anything beyond the companionship of the dance.

While he spun with her, both hands around her waist, listening to her breathless laughter, he felt a pang of sincere regret that he was not the man he pretended to be. For a time he put aside the man he'd become and fully assumed the character of the man he'd rather be, allowing the music to carry them both away. This free-spirited, foot stomping, breathless freedom epitomized the risk-taking life of the frontier itself. Here anything seemed possible, including fresh starts.

"Did 'ya see? Father won the pie baking contest!" Adam's eyes shone with the pride of it. "Come see the ribbon he won!"

Jonathan dutifully followed Adam to the tent where all the contesting foods were on display. Timothy stood next to his strudel engaged in animated conversation with two older ladies.

One of them, a lady with an extravagantly large, brimmed hat, leaned forward, speaking in conspiratorial fashion. "Now, Mr. Hindricks, you want to be careful about giving away any secrets. Sure as I'm breathing, next year there'll be five more just like yours."

"Oh, I'm not too worried about that. My mother shared her recipe with half the county, but no one could get it quite right. But really, cooking's a gift, and what good's a gift if you don't give it away?"

The hat lady touched his arm lightly with her hand, scrunching her nose as she said, "Well, you, Mr. Hindricks, are a gift to Snowberry. We're so grateful that someone finally come along to knock Mrs. Townsend plumb off her throne!"

Both ladies giggled like school girls as they walked away.

"See, Jonathan? It's the top prize!" Adam beamed at his father, touching the ribbon as though it were a precious artifact.

"Congratulations, Timothy. It's good to know I'm not alone in my good opinion of your cooking."

"Well, not all approved." Timothy leaned over, speaking softly. "Heard there were a few ladies who took objection to my strudel, complaining that it shouldn't be judged as a pie. Suppose that's understandable. But the lady that told me said it was the young lady doctor who made the decision to keep it in. That was nice, but I fear she might have made herself some enemies as a result."

Jonathan drew an amusing picture in his mind of the petite young doctor going toe to toe with some of the town's elite upper class. She'd be looking up their noses as they looked down at her. While the thought definitely amused him, he wondered if her independent spirit might be creating some unnecessary enemies. On the frontier, that was never wise.

"Father, can we go watch the shooting competition now?" Adam had caught sight of the stream of picnickers heading to the far side of the field. "I heard the mercantile donated some ammunition for the winners. Maybe you could enter, Jonathan."

"Adam, I hardly think you should be telling a man his own business." Timothy rested his fists on his hips and frowned down on his son.

"No need to scold the boy. He's just fired up with the devilry of competition right now." Jonathan gave Adam's elbow a nudge. "Come on then, let's go watch the fun."

All three joined the crowd of onlookers stretched out along the edge of the prairie. Targets had been set up for rifles and pistols. The first competition would be with pistols. Out of the corner of his eye, Jonathan saw Kat Meriwether and her father approaching the line of spectators. Not far to her side was Ethan Hall. He also noticed that Kat's hand was linked in her father's arm, not the young man's. That gave him some satisfaction.

The competitors formed up in groups of three. Six targets per shooter, best of six advanced to the next tier of competition. While most of the crowd focused on the accuracy of shots, Jonathan studied the style and intentionality of each man. He found the variety of pistols interesting and even more amazing were the abilities of many shooters to compensate for their antiquated weapons. Some of the antiques used were worthy of note, making the accuracy of their shooters more impressive.

It came as no surprise that Ethan Hall advanced to the line to try his luck. Although he appeared casual enough as he waited for the others to ready themselves at the line, Jonathan suspected the young man was more than casually acquainted with the gun he wore so comfortably at his hip. When he successfully won out over the others in his group of three, he modestly stepped aside for the next group. But Jonathan had seen, probably more than anyone else, the man's expertise with the weapon. He was quick and he was deadly accurate.

"Ah, come on Mr. Winthrop. You could beat them all. I've watched you practice at home. You're fast! And I've never seen you miss, not once! You could win!" Adam's eyes were wide with his appeal.

Jonathan just shook his head. "I appreciate the vote of confidence." He pulled a piece of taffy from his pocket, handing another one to Adam. "But shooting just isn't a thing I do for sport."

Jonathan knew the smell of trouble brewing, and the town was rank with it. This was no time to be showing one's hand. This was a time for staying low, staying quiet, and most important, staying watchful. The real players, whoever they were, would be doing just the same.

The explosion of gunshots snapped him out of his ruminations. What was he thinking? He wasn't a lawman. If there was a fight coming, it wasn't his. He'd most likely be gone before it started, moving on, maybe Oregon Territory or as far as Canada. He unwrapped another piece of taffy and stuffed it in his mouth, casting a thoughtful look in the doctor's direction.

From where he stood, he could see her furrowed brow. Something had made her unhappy, or was it uncomfortable?

He also noticed that her father was no longer beside her. A short distance behind her, another man, one whose flat face and square body looked vaguely familiar, was working his way through the crowd heading directly toward her. Jonathan watched the swagger in the man, the vacuous expression of one who had probably been drinking.

Kat apparently saw him too, moments before he spoke to her. Jonathan saw her body stiffen into a defensive posture— a posture that told him she knew the man, but more importantly that she didn't like him. Jonathan watched, his dark eyes shaded, obscured by the brim of his hat.

Nathaniel Meriwether came up behind her and Jonathan heard him call out her name. When Kat turned, Jonathan watched her posture relax. Nathaniel was carrying a rifle which he handed to Kat. He saw her brown curls shake as she declined some suggestion by her father. The younger, flat faced man spat out some words that Jonathan couldn't hear. Directly, he forced his way to the front of the spectators.

Light, unenthusiastic applause lifted from the crowd as the winner of the pistol competition was announced. It was awarded to Ethan Hall. Jonathan was not surprised. His face creased into a half-smile, devoid of real satisfaction.

Fewer in number were the competitors for the rifle event. Doc Meriwether had apparently won the argument with his daughter. She stepped to the line with the first group. The targets were several yards farther out this time. Ten shots. Ten tries. Kat Meriwether struck true on all ten, so did one of the men. The flat-faced man with the crooked nose was in the second group. Ten for ten.

Twelve competitors narrowed to just three. The flat-faced man leaned in close to Kat, speaking to her. Her shoulders stiffened again, but she didn't turn her head, and whether she gave a reply, Jonathan could not determine. Kat again shot ten of ten, as did the flat-faced man. The third competitor missed one. So, it was down to two.

Jonathan observed Kat's form with admiration. She was steady, obviously sure of herself. There was not the slightest suggestion of nerves or rushed performance. Ten times, she lifted, pulled the trigger, levering quickly another round. The flat-faced man, despite his inebriated state seemed quite capable of focusing on his target. Perhaps he was one of those individuals who is in a perpetual state of mild inebriation, capable of functioning better while under the influence of a small amount of alcohol. He'd actually ridden with a Ranger who swore he shot more accurately with a shot of whiskey under his belt.

When both of them shot ten for ten, the targets were moved another 50 yards. At this point, Jonathan caught sight of Ethan, his face appeared strangely flushed, his body language screaming his irritation with something. At first, Jonathan thought it must be Kat's participation in the competition, but dismissed that on closer observation. It was the flat-faced man with whom Ethan Hall had an issue. Moving closer to the line, he said something to the flat-faced man that caused him to turn. There was a look there of familiarity, of authority to sub-authority. Hall was unhappy with him. For what?

Adam blew out a breath between his teeth, an attempt at a whistle. "She's some shot, huh, Mr. Winthrop?"

Timothy moved closer to Jonathan. "Sure don't like the look of that fellow she's shooting against. There's something . . . I don't know, not right about him."

Jonathan glanced over at Timothy whose face mirrored his concern. The man was no fool. Somehow, that made Jonathan feel a bit better that he was not alone in his apprehensions for this community, and for the doctor specifically. That made Jonathan glance over at Nathaniel. The man was rubbing the back of his neck, concern spread wide across his face, lips tight. Jonathan imagined that he was in that moment regretting ever fetching that rifle. No doubt he knew the flat-faced man.

His focus on Nathaniel Meriwether's face caused him to miss the final shots. The applause this time was an eruption of enthusiastic support for Kat's victory. He turned back in time to see a crowd of both men and women patting her on the back. The flat-faced man was pushed to the back of the crowd. But Jonathan noticed that Hall had taken him firmly by the arm, pulling him away. That was interesting.

Jonathan excused himself from Adam and Timothy's side, hurrying off in the direction the two men had taken. He didn't have to go far before he saw them mounting up to ride out. Jonathan spun on his heel, racing to Jessie.

Dangerous Chemistry

KAT AND HER father sat on the grass at the edge of the field watching a group of men and boys playing a peculiar game of baseball. Each team seemed to be playing by a different set of rules. Neither seemed to match up with the two games she'd witnessed in Boston. But when they weren't arguing, they appeared to be enjoying themselves.

Kat took a sip of cool tea. She wished she could enjoy the afternoon, but her thoughts had been ambushed by the earlier events of the day. Liam had spoiled it for her, calling her back to their earlier lives of animosity. She'd thought such childish bickering would have been a thing of her past. Now it took on an added degree of ugliness.

Nathaniel glanced over at his daughter who had been quiet since the shooting competition. "I didn't know Liam would be entering the contest. I hadn't seen him in so long, I thought perhaps he'd moved on."

"I saw him earlier, last week in fact." She drew her knees up to her chest and leaned a cheek against her hand, looking sideways at him. "He said some fairly unpleasant things. It seemed at the time a threat. I don't know. Maybe it was my imagination."

Nathaniel closed his eyes, uttering a low groan.

"What is it, Papa?"

He shook his head slowly, casting his gaze toward the distant snow-capped mountains stretching north. "I'm afraid we've got ourselves into a terrible situation, Kat. Liam, Gilford Hall, and now this new man...Gilford said something today that would be hard to take as anything less than a threat. I'm becoming more convinced he's a part of these stage robberies, using his guise as a lawman to control the road to and from the mines."

The frustration that had been building burst from her with a fury. "Why doesn't someone suggest actually holding an election for sheriff instead of just standing by and allowing him to take control? This town was founded by some very strong, self-determined men. I don't understand why they aren't standing up to him."

Nathaniel shrugged, looking chagrined. "We all got old."

As Kat looked into her father's weary eyes, she regretted her tone that sounded more like an indictment than she'd intended. These were the men she'd looked up to all her life, men who'd carved a civilized community from a wild frontier. In less than three decades, this valley had been transformed from a battleground to a pleasant place to raise a family. Yes, there were still skirmishes with renegade Indians and the constant threat of sickness and drought, but they had brought a form of civilization that she'd grown up expecting to last for many more decades. They had established law and order. Now, it seemed they were moving backward.

"What are we going to do?" She left the question hanging there for a while, wanting to hear him supply the answer as simply as he'd supplied them to her as a child. *Fix it, Papa. You are the one I depend on.*

Nathaniel heard the disappointment in her voice. "I don't know, honey. Wish I did."

Kat saw the tear hanging in the corner of his eye and reached over to touch his hand.

"Did you know that Jonathan Winthrop was once a Texas Ranger?" he asked.

Kat's eyes opened a bit wider; hearing the rumor from her father added weight to its credibility. "Rumor, or did he tell you?"

"I asked him. He seems young to have quit a job like that."

Kat shifted her gaze to the game, where three of the older men were arguing with a youth about his uncertain status on third base. "And you are wondering if he might be the answer." She said it without a hint of how she viewed the solution.

"Maybe. Maybe, if we asked him, explained our situation."

A vision of Jonathan's somber gray eyes, clouded by some hidden pain, came clearly to her mind. Undoubtedly that haunted expression gave evidence to the reason the man had walked away from his profession. What right did she or anyone have to ask him to open the wound?

Trailing someone without his knowledge was one of Jonathan's many skills. He was legendary for it, trailing men for days, then suddenly appearing in their campfire light, a warrant for their arrest in his hand. Sometimes the warrant was served. Sometimes not. But he always found his man and brought him in, except once.

Keeping a short distance behind the men, Jonathan managed to keep up with them without giving his presence away. It helped to have a horse with as much experience as Jessie. A few miles from town, Ethan Hall halted his horse, calling to the flat-faced man. There was a dangerous moment of silence as they faced each other on the shadowed edge of wood. Then Hall spoke low with the tremor of scarcely bridled rage.

"You were given instructions to stay at the cabin, until we came to you."

"And I told you. You ain't my boss!"

"You think my father is going to ride out and show he has any connection with you? You're a known troublemaker. He has to keep up some kind of pretense to be legit. I'm taking a risk being seen with you!"

Jonathan sensed the volatility of the flat-faced man, wondering that Hall was pushing him this hard.

Hall pressed the point. "We won't be here much longer. This town isn't going to roll over, despite what my father thinks. So just sit tight. You and Noah stay in the cabin, until I come for you. We'll light out with what we have, then set up somewhere else. But you have to give me more time to convince my father."

Reeling back in his saddle, the flat-faced man gave out a dangerous laugh. "You're such a papa's boy, aren't you? Your papa has no intention of leaving this valley. And as for these town's folk takin' him on, well you're as blind as my great granny. That just ain't goin' to happen. I grew up here, remember?" He took a breath before starting in again. "The ones you need to be concerned about are that girl and her father. The *doctors*." He spit out the word like a curse. "If they blab what they suspect happened with the guard, the game's up, little boy. All the pieces are goin' fall down on your head."

Hall answered him in a soft voice, eerily devoid of any emotion. "I've got it under control." Weren't those the words he'd heard his father say?

"You think so? Well, I could take care of her. Just give me the word, Hall, and I'll take very good care of her."

The pieces were in place, the corners, the edges, were all in place. Jonathan knew that a few missing pieces from the middle didn't make that much difference. How they'd done what they'd done, where they'd taken their stolen goods, didn't matter. He knew the players now, and it all seemed too horribly familiar.

He waited until the flat-nosed man, the man he'd called Liam, was gone. He waited as the younger Hall turned his horse's head back to town.

He had it under control. The truth that Jonathan knew from experience was that neither of them had it under control. He was beginning to doubt that anyone ever would or could. Fate or Providence always had its say in the end. Jonathan backed Jessie off the trail, following a game trail back to Snowberry. If it were within his power to do so, he would do his duty, not as a Ranger, but as a man who had the gift and the call to protect the innocent.

Ethan combed his hair with nervous fingers, dusted his clothes with his hat, and put on his most appealing smile, the one he used to bait. He located her near the stand erected for the musicians and strode purposely to her.

Kat had taken Adam's hand, before Ethan could approach her. She smiled encouragement into his eager face. Knowing it was his first, she led him through the dance. She could see that he was smitten with her and so she treated his attraction seriously, not wishing to wound his tender heart. They danced, awkwardly at times, as Adam tried to find his feet and match them to the rhythm of the tune.

Ethan waited. His hands seemed restless, clenching and unclenching, almost in rhythm to the music. He'd always hated waiting. His certainty at controlling the situation was in jeopardy. As he watched her, he had to fight the voice within telling him to run. With a volatile man such as Cahill in the picture, his father wasn't even in control. If he were to get on his horse right now, he might be able to get to the cabin without Liam seeing him. Maybe he'd take at least one bag of gold before heading out. California might be a good place with a man of his talents. There were still places there where he might be safe from those who knew him.

The music ended. Adam bowed to Kat and she curtsied to him. Ethan quickly maneuvered around a pair of laughing youths. In his haste he caught his heel in the young lady's dress hem. When he'd extracted himself, he had to relocate Kat amidst the other dancers. Spotting her, he started in her direction.

Kat watched Adam return to the table where his father was waving him over for dinner. There was a light tap on her shoulder, and she turned, half expecting to see Ethan Hall again. When she looked up at Jonathan, a little gasp involuntarily escaped her lips. She laughed to mask her embarrassment at the reaction.

"Mr. Winthrop, I wasn't expecting to see you. My father thought he saw you leave." Kat worked to restore her composure, which seemed constantly at risk when she was anywhere near him.

"I did."

"Well, I'm glad you came back." *Oh, what a stupid thing to say.*

The music lifted again to a slower beat. Standing at her side, Jonathan made no attempt at further conversation. She wondered if she should ask him to dance, and then thought better of it. Suddenly, Jonathan seemed to thaw from his frozen state and come to himself. "Would you care to dance, Dr. Meriwether?"

"Only if you call me Kat. Most of the townspeople can't remember to call me Dr. Meriwether, and I doubt they ever will. Most of them still think of me as the tomboy they once knew. It's hard to shake those impressions. My father will always be Dr. Meriwether. I think I might one day persuade them to call me Dr. Kat. I can live with that." She was talking fast, unable to slow her tongue as it raced ahead of her purposeful, practiced restraint. What had happened to the discipline of recent years? Hadn't she overcome her impulsive youth, acquiring through her aunt's guidance the less opinionated demeanor of a lady, carefully measuring her thoughts before expressing them?

He gave her a wan smile, but she felt the warmth of it down to her sore toes. "Then Kat it is. But then I suppose you should call me Jonathan."

He extended his hand. She slowly placed her fingers in his. His other hand slipped naturally around her waist, the warmth of it spreading up to her neck and into her cheeks. *Oh, please no blushing.*

The fiddler slowed his pace as the dancers tired of their more gymnastic reels. Jonathan led her confidently in and out of the other dancers. He held her with such firmness, causing her to feel at times that her feet were scarcely touching the ground, his arms alone carrying her through the dance. They moved together, weaving effortlessly through couples revolving in their own worlds, like constellations of two. Faster than the rhythm of the music, faster than the spinning earth beneath her feet, her heart beat against her ribs at a most unhealthy rate.

Chemistry, she told herself, this was dangerous chemistry, the kind that could become unstable. This argument in her head, this warring of her body and her mind was something familiar. She'd fought it for four years and her mind had always won. But the pleasure of being held so firmly in Jonathan's arms, made her doubt that she would win it this time. She had an impending impression of danger here and at the same time an overwhelming sense of safety. It was similar to the safety she felt in her father's arms, but something more, something far better.

She felt the tingling warmth of his hand slide from her waist to her back, as he pressed her close to his chest. Now the pounding of her heart was compounded by the thumping of his, as if one was trying to speak to the other in some secret language unknown to the human ear. He turned with her in a tight circle, making her head spin, his chin now resting lightly on her head, his new growth of whiskers prickling her scalp. Closing her eyes, she yielded to his leading, trusting him to carry her through the dance.

The freedom of the reel she'd danced with Ethan called out the joyful exuberance of her youth, the eagerness to relish what life could bring. It was a dance she could have performed without a partner, dancing with life itself. But this was vastly different, stirring the passions long suppressed. Unlike the foot-stomping excitement of the first, this dance required a partner, a man such as Jonathan Winthrop.

Too soon, the music ended. Jonathan held her a moment longer, before stepping back, releasing his hold upon her. Her fingers retained the memory of the warmth of his hands for another moment, then the coolness of the afternoon returned to send a chill through her body. How much better it would be to stay in his warm embrace.

Looking up into his eyes, those somber dark eyes, she wondered at the terrible wound that had emptied them of joy. The doctor she'd been trained to be considered what remedy would cure him. What would heal the wounds? More than that, she wanted so very much to be the one to do it.

Jonathan pulled his gaze away from her, knowing this was the very distraction that he could not afford if he were to protect her. To keep his wits about him, he sensed his need to distance himself from her, away from her lavender scented hair and dark searching eyes. This had been unexpected, this charge of attraction that seemed to flow through every nerve ending.

From the corner of his eye, he glimpsed the young Hall leaning against the side of the church. His body conveyed nonchalance but his eyes were fixed upon Kat. As much as Jonathan wished to fade into the crowd, keeping his vigilance from a distance, this was not the time to leave her side. He brought his attention fully back to Kat. Aware that he didn't dare take her in his arms again, he extended his arm to her and asked, "Would you care to take a stroll, Dr. Kat?"

She smiled and wrapped her arm through his. "Just Kat."

Placing his hand lightly upon hers, he led her to the edge of the church lawn where the prairie began, stretching a mile to the river and another mile to the western foothills. The last rays of sunlight glowed in hues of orange and pink behind the distant mountain range, making the shadowed outline of peaks more distinct by contrast to the light.

He glanced behind to see if Hall had followed them. Catching no sight of him, he turned back to look down at Kat. Long fingers of soft light seemed to caress her face, slipping golden highlights through the locks of her hair. She looked up at him with her searching brown eyes. Embarrassed, he looked away.

Not trusting himself to look at her just now - not until his pulse had slowed, he said, "You must love your father very much to come back here. I'd have imagined there were many places with more to offer. . .towns that'd been grateful for a doctor."

Jonathan felt her eyes on him. She took her time in answering, making him wonder if he'd touched a nerve.

At last she said, "I do love my father. He's been my rock for all my life." She turned her face to the hills, her words faltering and strained with emotion. "I admire him more than any man I've ever met. He's kind and compassionate, smart and witty, and brave."

He heard the hesitation and glanced down to see the tension lining her young face.

"And yes, I . . . did have offers," she said softly. "I do. ."

Jonathan saw her slip a hand into the pocket of her dress, thinking he could hear the crinkling sound of paper as she did.

"It's complicated, isn't it? I used to think that becoming a doctor would be the key to every door I've ever wanted to open." Her fingers tightened on his arm. "It's just that I have a skill now. It's almost as though I don't possess it, but it possesses me. I'm not even sure that I have the right to say how it's used, because it's like a gift." Her breathing had changed, the words came spilling out, jumbled thoughts that had not been sorted and neatly filed. "If those skills are needed, do I have the right to say how or where? If they truly are a gift."

He waited for her to continue, but when she did not, he volunteered, "I'm not sure that it's wrong to stay or go as long as you use them."

Jonathan saw the turmoil that she was in, saw it in the tense lines about her mouth and felt it in the grip of her fingers on his arm. He didn't understand the specifics, the who or the why, but he understood the forces pulling on her. He understood them so very well.

"Oh my!" Kat took in a deep breath, looking away. "I'm so sorry. . .I don't know why. . ." She pulled away and wrapped both her arms about her, hugging her chest. She laughed lightly. "You are very easy to talk to. I think I've needed to say those things out loud. Coming back here. . .I wasn't prepared for the changes, I guess."

"What kind of changes?" He asked it, knowing some of them, assuming others.

She flung her hands out to the town. "The town has grown so much! It's doubled in size. My father's tired out. I can see it in his face, the weariness."

"Town's lucky to have a skilled doctor. Not many towns west of the Mississippi can boast to having one. Where I come from, there just weren't any. The big cities had them, but often-times it was Indian medicine that was the closest you could get to any doctoring or some snake oil salesman."

With the soft brush of her fingertips, Kat touched his arm again, creating a shock that sang through him. He mustn't allow these emotions to be stirred. They would only interfere with his ability to focus on protecting her.

Unaware of her effect on him, she continued, "But it's other changes that have me worried. Jonathan, I don't trust the sheriff or the men he has working for him. I know some of them. They were bullies when I was here, and *now* they're supposed to be protecting the townspeople?" She shook her head, her voice dripping with sarcasm.

"Wouldn't be the first time I've heard of a sheriff with a shady past." If he could get her to trust him and share what she'd learned that had the Hall's anxious, he might be able to put a few more of the pieces together. Low and quiet, he pushed his luck a bit. "But there's something else about this troubling you."

She hugged herself as though she were cold, but the warm breeze suddenly lifting across the valley belied the source of the chill. He saw the struggle in her face as she worked out her level of trust in him.

Kat tossed her head angrily. "One thing that I know *is* true, is that there's more violence now than before we had a sheriff. There've been fights in town. That never happened before. People are putting locks on their doors. It's the men that I know surrounding the sheriff that makes me suspect he's involved."

"I'm pretty sure that he'd say he took over the job because of the violence."

"Probably. But did you know that he wasn't even elected? And Father says no one wants to confront him about it." Fire flashed in her eyes. "Oh, if I were a man! If I were a man, I'd demand that there be an election so that the town could decide."

"And would there be any one of them willing to put himself in that position?" Jonathan asked softly.

Ignoring the question, she threw her arms around herself again. "And I wouldn't even be allowed to vote."

Jonathan wasn't holding any convictions one way or the other about women's suffrage, but he could definitely see her reason for frustration. If there wasn't a man with enough backbone to stand up to Hall, they'd just have to suffer the injustice of it. The consequences would inevitably follow. More disturbing was the threat he'd heard directed at Kat and her father, placing both of their lives in peril.

A sudden thought struck him that she was testing him. Did she know he'd been a lawman? Had she heard the rumors as well or had her father told her? Was she expecting him to confront Gilford Hall? Jonathan caught the movement from the corner of his eye and looked up sharply to see Nathaniel approaching. "Dr. Meriwether."

"I see you've been taking care of my daughter." Nathaniel winked at Kat as she reached for his arm, wrapping hers around his.

"My pleasure. We've been discussing...politics," Jonathan said.

"Oh my! I wouldn't have advised that. She's got some headstrong opinions," Nathaniel teased.

"Don't we all where politics are concerned? Don't think women are alone in that."

"Suppose you're right about that. Kat's been keen on the subject ever since she read an essay by Lucretia Mott a year or so before she left for Boston. She started reading through newspapers like other women might study that magazine, *Ladies' Home Journal.*"

"And who gave me the article to read?" Kat tugged on her father's arm, shooting back a teasing, narrow-eyed challenge.

Nathaniel shrugged and grinned.

Jonathan said, "An educated man, like yourself, was bound to raise a child with strong opinions. Seems a few men could use their brains a bit more when forming their voting opinions. I've seen too many votes cast in exchange for a mere glass of whiskey. Think a woman's vote might not be so easily bought."

"Why, Mr. Winthrop, I'd never have figured you for an advocate of women's rights." Kat delivered him the warmest of smiles, with just a hint of humor.

"Well, ma'am, I'm not too certain of that. I'm just calling it as I see it. And I've met a fair number of men that vote without giving much thought to why or who they're voting for."

Kat's smile touched her eyes. "Thank you for that, and thank you. . .for the dance." She paused before adding, "And the conversation."

"We'd love to have you join us for dinner sometime," Nathaniel said, then looking at his daughter's horrified expression, he added, "I'll cook."

"I'd be privileged. A man who's traveled as much as me, catching a good meal is something worth riding the hills for. Thank you."

Jonathan remained where he was watching them walk away. He waited for a short time, scanning the crowd for Hall. Watching his back as well as theirs, he followed them at a short distance, staying in the shadows.

After a short walk of a few hundred yards, he noticed that someone was indeed following them. On the opposite side of the street, hidden in the shadow of two buildings was the younger Hall, the man who *had it under control*. As if uncertain, the man stood there for a few minutes until Nathaniel and his daughter had started up the hill to home. After a time, he turned away. Jonathan waited until he saw him mount up and ride in the opposite direction. Then he waited at the base of the hill until he'd seen Kat and her father enter their home and lights appear within.

He brought his hand up to pinch the bridge of his nose. Pulling his hand away almost as though he'd been stung, he looked at his fingers where the scent of lavender still clung. Remaining professionally distant would be difficult this time. Beyond the sweet fragrance of lavender, there was something about Kat Meriwether that lingered with him still.

Exhausted as she was, all Kat wanted to do was take off her ridiculous corset and tight shoes, then crawl beneath the covers of her bed to sleep. But sleeping did not come easily. To make it all the more frustrating, it wasn't life choices, concern for her father, or even the threat of impending disaster that fueled her insomnia. Those reasons would have been excusable, tragically laudable even. No matter how much she pinched her ear, she couldn't shake the pleasurable memory of Jonathan Winthrop.

She tried all the techniques that had been a part of her self-government, her discipline of higher cognitive reasoning over petty temptations. She tried thinking of those things she did not approve of in the man. There were none. She liked the musky scent of him, of leather, and horses, and the soap that lingered from his last shave. The rich tone of his voice, the measured cadence of his speech, the gentle way his hand held hers only improved her opinion of him. She liked the way his clothes stretched across his broad shoulders, the easy manner in which he controlled all that muscle and sinew to hold her tight to his chest without crushing her. And, blast it all, she even liked his politics!

In his arms she had felt so safe. In all her self-sufficiency that was one strength she never felt she possessed. She never felt completely safe. It riled her that although she might be able to win a debate, or even win a shooting contest against a man, she knew her vulnerability as a woman. But in Jonathan's arms, she felt her resolve to be completely self-reliant dissolve.

She had faced three smiles that day that held a quality of danger. One smile sprawled across the face of her childhood enemy, Liam. She wouldn't soon forget his threat. The other smile, smooth and inviting, belonged to the handsome Ethan Hall. But the most dangerous smile of all was that which touched the serious eyes of Jonathan Winthrop. His gentle smile posed the greatest peril of all. When the corners of his mouth lifted, the warmth that radiated from his heart was like the rising of the sun on a cold Idaho morning. Jonathan Winthrop was indeed a dangerous man.

A Habit of Mistrust

NOAH STANTON HAD been Liam's shadow since he'd been old enough to ride a horse, which was not long after he'd learned to walk, which was shortly after his mama had taken off his diapers, letting him shift that out for himself. Most people didn't even notice Noah unless he was standing in the proximity of Liam, even though he stood a head taller. His father had told him there wasn't a thought in his head that hadn't first been rattling around in Liam's. So, when Liam hatched a plan to take the gold they'd stashed behind the cabin and light out, of course Noah went along with it. The fact that Gilford Hall might do very bad things to them never resolved itself into a thought in Noah's head, because Liam confidently declared that they could get away with it.

Two pack mules and four horses had been *acquired* from a ranch outside Lake City. The plan had no finesse to it. Neither man possessed enough gray matter between them to devise anything that might even warrant the name *plan*. They were just going to load the saddle-bags with as much as the mules could carry and leave. The closest thing that resembled a plan was that they had a destination of Oregon Territory. How they themselves might avoid being victims of a robbery, or where they could find an assay office and sell the gold without raising questions had not been a topic of conversation.

"Did anyone ask you why you needed so much truck?" Liam asked Noah as he carried bags and boxes into the cabin while Liam sat on the sagging porch watching him.

"Nah. They just thought I was goin' huntin' in the mountains. I told 'em I heard there was a pack o' wolves up Mount Baldy and I was goin' to bag me a few and come down and sell the hides for a stacka' gold. I told 'em I might even try to snag me a bear, maybe two. That's why I needed all them supplies." Noah looked quite pleased with himself.

"You told 'em all that, did 'ya? Seems you did a might more talkin' than I told you to. Dang, Noah! What was you thinkin'?" That was a rhetorical question, of course, and Noah stood with his mouth agape.

"Well, it don't matter much. I'm just quit of this place. I'm tired of that pretty boy, Ethan, telling me what to do! And I ain't so sure that new man, Cahill, ain't got his own ideas about stealing the gold."

The sun had set before they could finish sorting out the essentials that they'd need and those items that Noah had simply taken a fancy to. Not having carried that much money at any time in his life, the temptation was too great not to buy a few extras that caught his eye, like a full tin of lemon drops and another of black licorice. Liam conceded that he could take with him as much as he could carry in his pockets but no more. So, while they packed up the saddle-bags, Noah continued to stuff copious amounts of lemon drops and licorice into not only his pockets, but his mouth.

Liam tugged on the halter of the second mule, attempting to pull him closer to the cellar in back where the gold was stashed. He was anxious to be loaded and on their way before sunrise, thinking Ethan and the rest of them might be coming at any time. As much as he hated the sheriff's cock of a son, he had no desire to face him with a gun. Liam wasn't *that* good. Maybe if he could ambush him, he could take him out with his rifle, but that wasn't in his plan. He just wanted to be shut of Snowberry for good. He'd been looked down on too long by her good citizens.

Unfortunately, for both men, Ethan had decided to bring the promised supplies on this night. Frustrated by the day's events and his lack of success in getting information from Kat Meriwether, he decided a ride might be just what he needed. As it turned out, it was not.

His horse and the one he led packed with supplies stepped into the cabin's clearing just as Liam finished loading the last pack. Liam's head snapped up. From over the back of the mule he watched warily as Ethan approached the cabin. With eyes locked on the man, he pulled the pistol from the holster at his hip.

With the light of a nearly full moon, Ethan cautiously scanned the area, a habit of mistrust developed over the years working with men who trusted him as little as he trusted them. Riding in with his rifle balanced on his lap, his hand resting on the trigger guard, the muscles in his lower back tensed with each step. Tied to the porch post both men's horses stood saddled, pawing impatiently at the ground. Liam and Noah may have been lazy but both treated their horses better than family. They wouldn't leave them tacked up unless...

Ethan swung his head, straining to see past the shadows to either side of the house. Slipping from the saddle, he positioned himself so that his horse shielded him from anyone in the house. The fact that no one had stepped out to greet him only increased his uneasiness. The horses gave evidence that the men were still in the vicinity and they most likely were aware of his presence since he'd done nothing to make a stealthy approach, something he wished he'd thought to do.

"Liam! Noah! Come on out and see this fine box of whiskey I brought you." Having announced his presence, he brought the rifle barrel up, slowly chambering a round as he did. A movement in the shadow to the right of the cabin drew his eye.

"Liam, that you?" Ethan recognized the man's stoop-shouldered bulk. "I brought some supplies for you and

Noah." He kept his voice even, casual, but the rifle in his hands belied his tone.

"Might neighborly of you." Liam's voice spoke from the shadows, simmering with anger.

"Surprised you haven't tended to your horses. That's not like you." Ethan sought to buy some time to assess the situation. He'd feel easier knowing where Noah was. "Hey, Noah! Come help me carry in your supplies."

"He's busy." Ethan could see the shadowed figure toss his head to the side. "Privy."

"Mr. Ethan?"

Ethan's gaze shifted to the left of the cabin, where Noah stepped out of the shadows, slack-mouthed, leading a pack mule.

Well, this was the least favorable scenario he could have imagined, flanked in the dark. Ethan continued to feign ignorance of the obvious intentions of the two men to head out. The packs on the mule certainly didn't suggest their departure was simply to take off without compensation. "What's going on, Liam?"

"I've had enough of you and your father! Me and Noah got plans of our own," Liam snarled back. As he did, he side-stepped to the protective cover of the cabin's western wall. "Now you, just head on back to your daddy."

Ethan could see the glint of moonlight off Liam's revolver. "Liam! You'll never get away with it." He didn't shout it. He simply stated the obvious fact.

From his left, Ethan watched Noah step forward, apparently unaware of the dangerous position he had moved into. "Ethan, why are you here?"

"Noah, get back!" Ethan shouted this time, worried that Noah would soon block his view of Liam. He tried again to reason with the man. "Liam, you know my father will never stop chasing you. He'll track you down."

Pulling up the mule, Noah turned to look in the direction that Ethan now pointed his rifle. "Liam? We ain't gonna shoot anyone else, are we?"

Liam's voice from the deeper shadows called out, "Noah, you simpleton, get out of the way!"

Ethan scanned the shadowed edge of the clearing for Liam. All he could do was hope to take some shelter of his own on the opposite, eastern wall of the cabin. He ran past Noah and the unhappy mule, sliding behind the edge of the porch. Laying his head back against the log wall, he cursed softly; this was the out-of-control he'd feared. He'd managed to extract himself from worse situations by using his persuasive skills. He tried again. "Liam, take a sack of gold and you and Noah head out. You can set yourself up in a nice town and live pretty good." Ethan didn't want to do this. He was sick of the whole thing. If he could just head out on his own, he would. An owl hooted from a nearby pine, laughing at him. His father wouldn't let him go either. "Liam, I don't want to fight you."

A sudden movement to his right brought him to his feet too late. He swung his rifle a moment after the flash from Liam's pistol sent a bullet ripping into Ethan's stomach.

Ethan fired, striking Liam squarely in the chest. The man fell backward with the impact, crying out. Ethan dropped his gun and sagged to the ground.

Noah came at a run, kneeling by his friend's side, a look of disbelief washing over his face. "Liam? Liam? You dead?"

Ethan watched as Noah picked up Liam's gun, staring at it with a vacuous expression.

"You killed him, Ethan." Noah stood and walked toward Ethan, the gun hanging limp in his hand.

Perhaps he could still survive this. Noah wasn't a killer like Liam. He spoke calmly but with labored breath. "Noah, I need for you to go get my father. Tell him I've been hurt."

Noah shook his head slowly. "I can't do that. He'd kill me."

Ethan felt himself losing focus. He had to get through to this man. "Noah, I'll explain that it was Liam's idea, and you had nothing to do with it. Noah! Look at me!"

Noah dropped the gun and knelt down gaping at the blood pouring from between Ethan's fingers. "You're hurt bad, Ethan."

"Yes, Noah. Go get help. Please." He closed his eyes, passing into unconsciousness.

As Noah rode down the trail, he had a thought that was all his own. It took root in his mind and he watered it with words to keep it fresh in his memory. "I'm goin' to get Ethan help. I'm goin' to get the doctor and get Ethan help so he won't die."

The Wound

LEANING CLOSER UNTIL she could feel the man's breath against her cheek, Kat strained to hear the words he labored to say. With so little breath left in his blood-filled lungs, the word hissed from his lips as a single gasp. "Hall."

Kat woke with a start, sitting up, pulling the covers to her neck with clenched fists. *Was that what he'd said?* Had she misunderstood that last word breathed into her ear by the dying man? She shivered and reached for the quilt she'd kicked off the bed earlier in the night. Wrapping it around her shoulders, she slid her legs from under the sheets and placed her bare feet on the cold floor. She gasped with the chill. Immediately her mind cleared, but her heart continued to beat a rapid cadence within her chest.

She padded to the window, pulling back the linen curtains to look down on the darkened streets in the town below.

One light burned in the boarding house window where she presumed the cook, Mrs. Carter, was already up and making fresh bread for the guests. Another glow came from the back rooms of the mercantile. Perhaps Mr. Forester's rheumatism was flaring in his knees again, giving him trouble with sleeping.

Like a hospital chart hanging from the end of her patient's bed, Kat mentally *read* the symptoms of her town's problems. Violence had increased. People were afraid to confront the one man who declared he was here to protect the town. Robberies were continuing in spite of his growing contingent of 'law keepers.' A guard, with fresh bruises and a gunshot wound only hours old had suddenly reappeared at the sight of the robbery a full day later. The Frenchman's cabin was now occupied in easy striking distance of the wagon road to the mines. Somehow, even with the changing routes, the robbers knew where to strike.

She'd read the symptoms and had she been in the hospital she would have formulated a diagnosis and a plan. But the results of her observations were inconclusive, making a plan more difficult. Shaking her head with both weariness and frustration, she realized again why she hadn't spoken to Jonathan about her concerns. Everything she knew or suspected was purely circumstantial, and no court of law would use any of it as evidence to convict anyone of wrongdoing. But the suspicions continued to gnaw at her.

Still gazing out the window toward Snowberry, she saw a horse and rider riding in fast through the dark streets, continuing to the trail leading up to the house. With the illumination of moonlight, the identity of the rider became clear a few feet from the house. Josie's husband, Simon, jumped from his horse and ran up the two steps to the front door. Kat answered before he had a chance to knock twice.

Riding fast up to the McCurry house on Blue along the moonlit trail gave Kat a chance to focus on something other than her concerns for the town in general and shift her attention to the happier advent of new life. Four hours later, with very little help from Kat, Josie delivered a beautiful girl, healthy and absolutely perfect in every way. It was Kat's first delivery on her own, and Josie's fourth.

"Well you were certainly right when you said you brought your babies into the world fast. I barely made it here in time. If I'd have delayed an hour, you would've been up making me a cup of tea." Kat laughed as she stood at the sink giving the youngest member of the Simon McCurry family her first bath. She knew that frontier wisdom advised against such things but the community would have to accept that with Dr. Kat Meriwether superstitions and old wives' tales had met their match.

Josie sat up in bed looking weary but content. Wrapping the infant in the rosebud blanket, Kat carried her back to the bed. Instantly, she was nursing at Josie's breast making her own contented sounds. Kat stroked the infant's downy soft head. "You do make beautiful babies, Josie. Have you decided on a name?"

"Of course. This one's Kathryn. We'll call her Katie for short so she's not confused with her Auntie Kat." Josie's joy was infectious, pulling Kat into it like she was wrapped in the same quilt of happiness.

Kat hugged her and the baby in one embrace. "That's sweet, Josie. Are you sure Simon agrees?"

"Oh, he doesn't care, just as long as he gets to name the next one Samuel." Josie chuckled.

"He's that sure, is he?" Kat asked.

"He's a very determined man."

"Let me make you some tea. Then I prescribe a long day off your feet, my friend," Kat said.

When Kat left Josie's house, sunrise was still an hour away. Simon protested against her starting for home before daylight, offering to ride with her when she would not be dissuaded. Kat insisted that Josie needed him more than she. So, he saw her off, warning her to be watchful.

Kat swung into the saddle. With a gentle squeeze of her knees, Blue started on the trail home. The world seemed to be holding its breath in anticipation for the arrival of the new day. How perfect, she thought, to deliver a baby at the start of such a glorious Idaho morning! As she emerged from the trees into a clearing that gave her a vista to the eastern range, she pulled up Blue. The distant snow-capped range stood backlit in a shade of blue-gray. She paused to think how the color matched that of Jonathan Winthrop's eyes.

Slipping from the saddle, she stepped forward to lay her hand on Blue's neck. The Morgan threw up her head as if questioning her. Kat surmised that she'd rather be back home in her barn with a pile of hay to occupy her morning. She rubbed her chin, crooning to her. "Oh, Blue, breakfast will wait, but this won't."

She hadn't been out this early in a very long time. Sunrise here had always been special to her, especially up in the high valleys. Sunrise in the city had a magic of its own, where the morning light gleamed against white marble in pink and orange, and rays illuminated lofty arched windows. Here, birds waited silently until the first rays broke behind the mountain before singing their songs of awakening. Before deciding the path it would take that day, the air itself seemed to take a deep breath and hold it. It was in that silent moment Kat thrilled, standing with creation, waiting for the revelation of the day ahead.

Light gave definition to the distant crags and peaks, just as it had the night before when she'd stood with Jonathan at the edge of the woods. Pale light began to bring the shadows below and around her into solid form. A tail flipped and Kat focused on the movement a little below her, lower on the flank of the mountain. The shadowed form resolved itself into a horse and rider, standing like statues. Both heads turned to the lightening sky.

Hues of pink and peach made a watercolor wash behind the mountain, projecting a pale glow on this side of the mountain on which they waited. Her eyes shifted from the point of most brilliant glow to the rider and back again. In an instant, light and warmth touched her face. She lifted her hand to her brow to gaze as light slid down the mountain to touch the rider and the horse below. Blue must have sensed the horse then, because she blew, nickering a soft call. Both the man and horse reacted at the same time. The man peered up at her, keeping his eyes upon her for a minute before turning his gaze back to the sunrise.

Although she could not make out the man's facial features hidden beneath his wide-brimmed hat, the sturdy bay was very recognizable. She took in a sharp intake of breath. He was here sharing this same sacred time in the quiet moments of dawn. She closed her eyes tight, wondering if she were dreaming. Perhaps Josie's baby, the ride here in the wee hours of the morning had been a part of the dream. She might yet awaken in her bed, warm and wrapped in her quilt. When she opened her eyes, the man and horse were gone. She mounted Blue and stood in the stirrups to get a higher perspective, searching the side of the mountain for any sign of them.

Minutes passed. Convinced that her lack of sleep had caused her to conjure him, she gazed down to the valley floor where thin light now washed it clean. Then he was there on the trail before her as if by some magic of the morning, outlined in the glow of sunrise.

"Good morning, Miss Meriwether." Jonathan's face shadowed by a night's growth of stubble looked almost sallow. His lips opened in a weary smile. "What brings you to the mountain at this hour?"

Suddenly aware of her own appearance, Kat felt self-conscious. She knew she must scarcely resemble the same girl he'd danced with the day before. "Josie McCurry gave birth last night to a little girl." She brushed a strand of hair behind her ear. "I've not had much sleep. I must look a fright."

His voice was so soft, that she scarcely heard the words. "Not at all. You look... lovely."

Kat felt the color rise to her cheeks. She quickly asked, "Do you usually rise so early?"

"No, ma'am, not quite so early to be here. Some of the steers wandered a bit yesterday while we were in town. We've been chasing them for a while, Adam and I."

"Oh, is he about?" She lifted herself in the stirrups to search the flank of the mountain.

"No, he headed back an hour or so ago. I just needed some time to think about things. Out here, the mind clears up."

She knew exactly what he meant. It's what drew her so often. Mornings were the best cure for a clouded mind.

"Are you heading back to town now?" he asked.

She sensed that this wasn't a casual question, considering his concern the last time he'd seen her travel home alone.

"Yes. I'm looking forward to a bath and a few hours of needed sleep. I think Blue is too. Well, maybe without the bath." She laughed nervously.

Jonathan asked, "Would you allow me to travel with you? I could do with picking up a few things from the mercantile."

She doubted the honesty of his excuse for traveling with her, but to refuse would be nearly akin to calling him a liar. She answered, "That would be fine."

The trail grew narrow, forcing them to ride single file with Blue leading the way. The sky turned from pale gray to a blush of pink as they traveled together in silence. Approaching the fork leading to town, the trail opened up. With a gentle pressure of his knee, Jonathan urged Jessie to catch up to the Morgan enabling them to walk side-by-side.

A few steps later and Kat broke the silence. "Father told me that you were a Texas Ranger before you came to our valley." She wondered at the wisdom of asking him, since he had not offered the information to her on his own. But his answer mattered.

"That's so."

Kat bit her lip as she considered whether she should push him for more explanation or respect his silence.

"I left the service," he volunteered.

"I see." She didn't, not really. His reply was far from an explanation. She regretted having brought up the subject.

"There was an incident, a kidnapping," he said. Kat glanced at him from the corner of her eye, watching his struggle to put words to the pain. She waited, holding her questions as she held her breath.

"There was a girl, a hapless, innocent pawn, but fate or Providence placed her directly in harm's way. I . . . underestimated the man who took her. Over-confidence in my abilities to measure the threat of a man led me to think I had the situation under control." He stopped. It was an uncharacteristically long speech for him, as though a rehearsed confession he might have once made. There was something about the way he said the word *underestimated* that sent an icy shiver down her spine.

He continued, each word carefully chosen. "Her survival depended on my playing the game better than the man who took her captive." His voice came flat from tight lips, eerily devoid of emotion. Kat pulled her coat close to her neck, suddenly chilled, listening to both the spoken and the unspoken explanation.

"I didn't."

Kat pulled up Blue's reins, tears suddenly welling up in her eyes.

Jonathan stopped as well. His face which had seemed sallow before, now looked ashen. She surmised that he hadn't told his story many times. Perhaps the pain it inflicted on him to confess it, reliving it, was too intense.

"I'm so very sorry, Jonathan. So sorry. . ." Her words came out hoarse, her throat tight. The sympathetic pangs of grief that pierced her were as much for Jonathan as for the unfortunate girl.

Now she knew. This was the wound he carried, a wound that had festered, refusing to heal, turning septic as years had left it untreated. But what could she do? With all her training to be a healer, what could she offer him? She doubted that her sympathy would do little for him. In fact, she surmised that he'd probably resent it. What she knew with certainty was that he desperately needed surgery to remove the cancer of self-condemnation.

"And you blame yourself for all of it." Kat did not say it as a question but a statement of fact.

"Of course." There was no bitterness in the statement. For him it was a statement of fact.

Kat reached across the space between them, stretching to touch his hand. Her fingers brushed his tight knuckles. "Doctors lose patients all the time. They miss things in their diagnosis. They fail to treat a wound effectively. They make mistakes and people die. If doctors walked away from what they'd been trained to do every time they lost a patient, there wouldn't be very many of us left."

"Have you?"

"Have I what?" she asked.

"Have you lost a patient?"

Kat closed her eyes, shaking her head. "No, not yet. But I dread the day it happens. I know it will come."

"Maybe we can have this discussion then, and it will mean something." Jonathan pulled his hand away from hers, touching his mare's flanks with his heels.

She sat unmoving, watching him ride on, his back stiff. "Jonathan! That's not fair. Why did you tell me?"

He pulled up Jessie, but didn't turn back. "I don't know."

Kat urged Blue forward until she was beside Jonathan again. "Please."

He looked at her with tortured eyes. "Please what?"

Taking a slow breath, she searched her mind for words to give him. The pain she read in his eyes was so intense, she felt the need to look away, but she didn't. She sorted through platitudes and rejected them all. At last she said, "In school, we had discussions with experienced physicians who had dealt with failure on even greater scales. One doctor told us of a child he'd thought had a simple tummy ache from eating too many sweets. But she had contracted cholera from a polluted creek. Before it could be contained, more than two dozen people died. It's a risky business, whether you are a doctor or a lawman. When people trust you and you let them down. . .It happens, Jonathan."

"I let my pride get in the way. I was good at reading criminal minds. But he read me better."

She could hear the candor in his confession, admiring him all the more for it. "You lost confidence in what made you good at your job." Kat wanted to touch him again, to comfort him, but she feared his reaction.

Jonathan sat back in his saddle, taking off his hat. With his other hand he ran his fingers through his hair in one long pass. Then he turned to her again, but his eyes were cast down to his hat still in his hand. "I know you want me to take on Gilford Hall. You don't have to dance around it."

Kat shook her head, her eyes wide. "That's not what I'm doing! I'm not trying to convince you of anything other than trying to help you see what happened in a different way. You did your best. I'm certain of it."

Jonathan chuckled mirthlessly. "You can't be sure of any such thing. The point is this. I'm not a lawman anymore. I handed in my star. I'm done." He drove his hat back onto his head, then lifted the reins.

"Jonathan, please."

He kept his eyes ahead of him, focused on the trail, closing out any argument against his own self-condemnation.

She could see, plain as day, how he'd lashed misery to himself as a form of penance.

He was right. She had hoped he'd confront Hall. Of everyone she knew, he was the man to do it. She was equally certain that if he did not step forward, the violence would escalate, changing her peaceful Snowberry forever. It would become like every other town that bordered nearly every gold and silver field. But it hurt her to think of the burden this decent man was carrying alone. How could she ask him to get involved in a battle for a town he hadn't claimed as his own?

"Need to see you home," he said, starting off at a trot, not waiting for her to say more. But she would not have said more, because she was fighting her own war where she was caught in the middle. Two sides warred a terrible battle, the good of the town versus the good of Jonathan Winthrop.

Jonathan slid from his saddle and walked the bay to the barn, following a few paces back from Kat and the blue roan.

Kat turned back at the door. "That's interesting. Dad must have gone out early this morning. The sorrel is gone and the buggy is still here. Must have been somewhere up in the hills where he'd have had trouble with the buggy. Maybe he left a note."

She led Blue inside and took off his tack. Jonathan stayed in the shadowed door frame his back to her while his eyes scanned the road leading to town. Kat could sense the tension in him from both his silence and his body. She gave the roan a quick brush down, then a generous breakfast of hay before crossing to the doorway to stand beside him.

With his gaze directed to the hills, he asked, "Did your father tell you about his conversation with Gilford Hall yesterday?"

Kat frowned as she tried to recall what he'd said. "I know that he said the man spoke with him, but nothing specific. Why?"

Jonathan rubbed his chin, blowing out a long breath. "He made a threat, against you and your father." He paused, then swung his head back to face her. "You can't trust him or his son."

She looked up, mouth slightly open, lost for words even though questions were bubbling within.

Jonathan put his hands on her shoulders, his grip as firm as his voice. "You've got to watch your back. Be alert. Come to me if you feel in danger." There was a fierceness in his eyes that frightened her.

"But I thought you wouldn't go up against Gilford Hall." She shook her head, confused and feeling a simmering burn of anger. She watched him slowly close his eyes, his jaw tightening. "I won't fight him for his job, but if I can keep him from hurting innocent people, I will."

His grip on her shoulders was painful now, and she pulled back, but he didn't let go. His lips parted, a look of something akin to surprise replaced the fierceness that had burned there a second before. In the next moment, his hands slid from her shoulders to her back and he pulled her tight to his chest. It was the most natural thing to do as she wrapped her arms around him. She yielded to his embrace and all the voices she'd trained to warn her away from such a situation were drowned out by the pounding of her heart, her pulse throbbing in her ears.

Slowly, as though he was afraid of breaking her, he brought his lips to hers. From such a man as he, she could scarcely imagine him capable of such a kiss, unhurried and tender. She slid her hands up his back, feeling the firm detail of his muscles with every nerve in her fingers. There was no anatomical dissection in her mind now. She was lost and found in the same moment.

That moment was far too brief. She felt the sudden chill as he pulled his warmth from her. He had placed his hands on her arms again, the confusion once more washing over his face. He shook his head once. "I'm sorry. I shouldn't have done that."

Stepping quickly away, he lifted himself effortlessly into the saddle. His eyes were focused on the hills for a long heartbeat before he looked down at her, his voice pleading. "Please, be watchful. Don't go anywhere without that rifle." Then he was riding away.

Kat brought her fingers to her lips. She'd heard the warning, but one thought floated above all the rest. *Why should he be sorry?*

Ten Kinds of Fool

NATHANIEL WASN'T SURPRISED that Kat had not returned home yet. Babies have their own schedule when it's time to be born and nothing anyone could do would change that.

He dressed and went to the kitchen to make himself a pot of coffee. Taking one of the medical journals Kat had brought home for him to read, he sat down at the table to wait for the water to boil. He hadn't read more than a page when he heard the fast approach of a horse up the road. Sighing, he closed the journal. A quick sip from his freshly brewed coffee was all he managed before the anticipated pounding started on his door.

Noah stood there looking gray and frightened. The words tumbled out on themselves, nonsensical. Nathaniel stepped onto the porch and placed his hands on the man's trembling shoulders.

"Slow down, Noah! Tell me what's happened."

"They've been shot, Doc! I think he's dead. And I think Ethan may be dying too."

"Who's dead?"

"Liam." The name came out choked.

"So, where's Ethan?" Nathaniel had already turned back into the house, heading to the examining room for his bag.

"He's up at the cabin above Schmidt's Valley. The old trapper's cabin."

Nathaniel mentally considered the possible reasons for the two men to have been in that remote area. Obviously, it was not some hunting accident if both were shot. With a sinking conviction, he knew that this had some connection to the recent wagon robberies.

Opening the drawer of his dresser to add another shirt to his kit, his hand brushed the cold barrel of his Colt pistol, the one he'd carried in the war. For a long moment he considered adding it to his bag. With what he knew and all he suspected, he very well might be walking into a very dangerous situation. He and Kat *had* been threatened. But he'd never used a weapon in his nightmare years of the war, why would he start now? Liam and Noah had been his patients from the time they could walk. Earning the town's respect as a healer had taken years of selfless and often thankless late-night visits to sick beds. No, he was a doctor. He'd been called and he'd answer as he always had.

Before heading out to the stable, he hesitated, wondering if he should write a note for Kat. But if this were a situation that was connected to the thefts, he didn't want Kat walking into it. Knowing her as well as he did, he knew she might not as easily leave her gun behind. He threw up an awkward prayer to a God he wasn't sure he believed in, then started off to the barn, where he quickly saddled up the sorrel.

"You are ten kinds of a fool!" Jonathan said it aloud to no one but Jessie, who nickered scornful agreement. "And who asked you? You'd have kissed her too if she'd looked at you that way. But then you'd kiss anyone who gave you a lump of sugar."

Jonathan pulled up just outside town, and lifted a hand to his chin. The stubble he felt there made him frown. "And I hadn't even shaved." He rubbed the back of his neck, feeling suddenly the lack of sleep. "I need some coffee."

The boarding house was open for breakfast. That sounded like the best idea he'd had all day. He found a table by the window with a good clear view of the town, one even allowing a view of the road leading to the Meriwethers' home. If anyone headed up there, he'd see them. Of course, he knew that they could come in from the mountain as well, but he couldn't exactly bunk there. He ordered coffee and pancakes.

Kat stayed on the porch for a while, her eyes following Jonathan as he rode down the hill to town. She wished she had the courage to call after him, to ask him to come back, to sit with her in the early morning light and just stay by her side. She wrapped her arms around her body, trying to recall the warmth she'd felt in his arms. Touching two fingers to her lips, she tried to bring the memory back. She squeezed her eyes shut, right hand instinctively drifting toward her ear. *No!* Thumb and forefinger hovered over her earlobe, poised to drive the memory of fierce, unexpected joy from her senses. She felt charged, as though a summer thunderstorm was brewing beneath her skin. Traitorously, her hand fell away.

She took in a deep breath. She breathed out. And then slipped the memory and the acknowledgement of desire into her pocket beside a worn letter.

The silence of a home hastily vacated is different than one left with forethought and intention. Clues are left behind, minutia in and of themselves, but as more are discovered, they build a worrying case for fear.

Kat found the coffee mug nearly filled, lukewarm, still on the table. She lightly touched the pot on the stove. It was still warm. *Hmm. He didn't leave that long ago. Wonder why he didn't leave a note.* She added fuel to the stove and went to her room to change her shirt and pants. It felt good to put on clean clothes and the smell of coffee improved her mood even more. Finding a muffin her father had purchased from the bake sale made her breakfast particularly pleasant. As she passed the kitchen table, her eye snagged on her father's coat, slung over the back of a chair. Odd for him to leave without it. It must have been a particularly urgent call.

She carried her mug out onto the porch where she gazed down into the town, the neat little houses, mostly painted white, gleaming in the early morning light. The town was stirring awake, someone was shaking out a rug, and a delivery wagon had just pulled up to the mercantile. This was still her town.

She frowned as Jonathan's words of warning drove away the impression of peace. *Watch your back.* Sheriff Hall knew she and her father suspected he was involved with these robberies. Suddenly, the sorrel's absence, the lack of a note, the lukewarm cup of coffee, the coat - these portents coalesced and drove a dagger of fear into her gut.

She put down her mug on the step and ran to the barn. Perhaps he'd told Mr. or Mrs. Forester where he'd gone. That was his habit after all. Blue wouldn't be happy about having her breakfast interrupted, but she'd feel better knowing where her father had gone. Worrying was pointless if a short ride to town would answer the question. Blue did protest the saddling before she finished her grass, but Kat stroked her neck and promised a half ration more.

When she walked into the mercantile, she found Mr. Forester at the counter measuring fabric for a customer. "Morning Kat! You're up early."

"Hello, Mr. Forester. Did Father come in this morning and tell you who called him out? Looks like he took off in a hurry since he didn't take the time to take the buggy."

"No. Haven't seen him in here. Anything wrong?"

Her heart dropped. She contemplated telling him of her concern, but checked herself. It could still indeed be her imagination and lack of sleep making her anxious. "Thank you, but it's fine." Kat turned, took a few steps, and stopped on the steps of the mercantile. Jonathan's bay was still tied to the railing in front of the boarding house. The temptation to run to him with this vague fear was so strong that she felt she fought against gravity.

Her right hand gripped the rough wood of the hitching post, grounding her. For the second time that day, she strove to strip away emotion and concentrate on the purity of inhalation and exhalation. Her heart steadied. Making her decision, she stepped into the saddle stirrup, swinging quickly up. She turned Blue toward home, racing to stay a breath ahead of fear and hesitation.

When the men entered the room, Jonathan looked up from his plate of pancakes floating in a pond of syrup.

A very square man wearing a suit coat and bowler hat walked in with two other men in similar attire, obviously business men since everyone else in the place was dressed like ranchers or farmers. "Well, I don't think we can just sit around and do nothing."

"And you're going to do something?" The taller of the three threw the square man a scornful look before sitting at a table next to Jonathan's.

"I didn't say that." The square man sat with his back to Jonathan.

"Well, he's right, but that's the trouble. No one's willing to face Hall, especially since he hired on that new man. I've never seen a more dangerous looking fellow. Jamison said he's known in Lake City for his speed with a gun. I can believe it! Thought those days were over. Lord-a-mighty! We're practically a state!"

The square man ordered a plate of two eggs, a slice of ham, and a stack of pancakes, then said, "We should elect a sheriff like other towns, not have someone dance in here and appoint himself!"

The tall man ordered biscuits and gravy and said, "Jamison heard the sheriff talking at the picnic that the only way to keep the town free of violence was to not allow anyone to carry a gun in town!"

The third man ordered coffee and said, "And how's he going to do that?"

The tall man said, "Jamison said that he's planning to make his deputies force anyone coming into town to check their weapons in at the office over there."

All three men made unique variations of a harrumphing sound of contempt.

"Well, people won't stand for it," the square man said.

The tall man said, "Jamison was talking to that new man that took over Schmidt's homestead, and he knows how to run a proper election. He once was on a committee back east that helped elect a mayor. He even served as president on a school board. He's a man of education, Jamison said."

Jonathan put down his fork and picked up his coffee mug, his attention now completely focused on the conversation.

"Maybe he'd run for sheriff," the square man offered.

"You gotta be good with a gun to be sheriff," the tall man said.

"Who said?" the third man asked. "Seems a smart man could do the job just as well, if he could hire himself some men who could shoot."

"Well, none of it matters if we can't get Hall to agree to an election, now does it?" the tall man quipped.

"Well, that's the truth. The thing is, this man, Hindricks, says a reasonable man would at least be open to it," the square man said.

"Don't think I'd call Hall reasonable." The third man snickered. "Anything but."

"Well Hindricks seemed bent on giving it a try, planned to talk to him soon, he said." The tall man sat back, arms folded across his chest.

The third man rocked his chair back and snorted. "That would be worth seeing."

Their food was brought to them and talking was suspended. Jonathan paid his bill and stepped out into the street, leaving his half-eaten breakfast on the table.

He felt it again, that sudden chill that warned him when a storm was coming, when peaceful resolutions would be overwhelmed with violence. *What was Timothy thinking?* He was too trusting to think he could reason with a man like Hall. The die had been cast when Hall had hired Cahill. He was making it clear to those who had ears to hear it, that any challenge to his authority would be put down with force.

Jonathan looked up the road in the direction of the Meriwether house. *Oh girl, what have you got yourself into?*

But Timothy had stepped into the same hornets' nest, with his optimism and good opinion of the intentions of men.

Jonathan knew different. Expect the worst and you won't be fooled.

He untied his bay and swung up into the saddle. With a kick to her flank, she started at a run. Jonathan felt a premonition of ill wind blowing clearly in the direction of Schmidt's Valley.

Nathaniel followed Noah up the narrow trail passing the homestead where Timothy, Jonathan, and Adam lived. There was a point in the trail where the trees thinned, giving Nathaniel a view of their cabin below. He could see a man on horseback speaking with a man standing just outside the cabin. He wondered if it was Jonathan, but from this distance he couldn't know for certain. He wished it were Jonathan, and he wished he could get word to him to go back down the mountain and stay with Kat until he knew everything was all right.

A few minutes more and they were emerging from the dense stand of pine into the small clearing with the sagging cabin. Nathaniel immediately took in the scene. Just behind the cabin stood two mules wearing what looked like heavy packs. One horse, still saddled, was grazing in the sunniest section of the clearing. Propped against the wall of the house was Ethan Hall, eyes closed, shirt stained red. In the dirt, a few yards away, lay the still body of Liam.

Nathaniel jumped down and handed his horse's reins to Noah. He first checked Liam's pulse, confirming Noah's fear that he was dead. Then he stepped up onto the porch and knelt by Ethan. He felt for a pulse. A light, but steady beat ticked beneath his fingertips. He stood and grabbed Ethan under his arms, turning his body so that he could ease him into a prone position. Ethan groaned softly.

Nathaniel hated gut shots. As a surgeon in the war, he'd seen enough for a lifetime. Men rarely survived them, but that was partially due to the triage pressure of treating those most likely to survive. With good care and prompt treatment it was possible to save them now. But odds of survival were still poor. He tore away Ethan's shirt and wiped the wound clean.

Ethan groaned again. Blearily, he looked up at Nathaniel, then to the side at the crumpled body. Nathaniel watched awareness return, like nausea hitting a seasick man.

Ethan squeezed his eyes closed, his words coming out raspy and soft. "Doc, you shouldn't be here."

Nathaniel laughed softly, though there was no real humor in his heart. "This is exactly where I should be. This is what I do."

Ethan lifted his hand, grabbing Nathaniel's wrist. "No! I mean it! You shouldn't be here. When my father comes and he sees you, he'll..." He closed his eyes for just a moment and spoke through clenched teeth. "He'll. . .he'll kill you."

"Because I know about his involvement in the robberies?" Nathaniel said.

Ethan hissed, "Yes." The guile so natural to him seemed to have drained out with his own blood.

"Ethan, this is what I do. I can't not do what I've been doing all my life. Let me do my job."

Ethan seemed confused but released Nathaniel's wrist. "Then patch me up and light out. Get back to your daughter. Protect yourselves. Maybe I can convince my father to leave now." Ethan sagged, eyes unfocused and drifting back toward the body, too weak to say more.

"Noah, look at me! Go get the sheriff. Tell him his son has been injured. We'll need help to get him down the mountain."

"But, Doc, he'll kill us both!" Noah whined.

Nathaniel looked up at Noah, his voice calm, steady. "Noah, this is the right thing to do."

Timothy saw Cahill ride in with Adam at his side. Adam was laughing as if in response to a joke Cahill had just told him. Timothy felt an alarming uneasiness seeing them together like that. He remembered the conversation Jonathan had relayed, the one in which he'd threatened Nathaniel and his daughter. He couldn't think of any good reason for the man to be in his valley. And more importantly, he couldn't think why he'd be in the company of his son.

"Morning, Father. Jonathan and I found those missing steers. We put them in with the others. Jonathan decided to take a ride into town. I met Mr. Cahill on my way over."

Timothy nodded to Cahill while addressing his son. "Why don't you put up your horse and go have your breakfast. Pancakes are on the table."

Timothy waited for Cahill to explain his presence while Adam led his own horse to the paddock.

"Mr. Hindricks." Cahill tipped his hat. "You've got a fine boy there. He seems to be educated, more than me anyway. This territory needs smart young boys like that to grow up into men who can build this territory into a state."

Timothy nodded, but held his tongue.

"I heard you was thinking of running for sheriff, that so?" Cahill asked casually.

Timothy couldn't help himself. He laughed. "Me? That's the first I heard of it."

"Folks say you've been talking about holding an election. They said you had experience with that sort of thing." Cahill took off his hat and pulled a hand through his slick hair.

"Yes, I do, and yes, some men were talking about it at the picnic, but I never offered to run. That's ridiculous."

Cahill put his hat back on his head and cocked his head to the side, staring at Timothy for a long moment. "Well, I'm glad to hear it. That doesn't seem like a good idea. Seems you have enough to do running this place and looking after that smart boy of yours. Would be a shame to have something happen to him riding out there alone. This can be a mighty wild country."

Timothy rolled his hands into fists, his arms rigid at his side. "I think you should leave my place, Mr. Cahill." He said it low with an unmistakable cadence of finality.

"I will, Mr. Hindricks. I will. Glad we had this little talk. Good day." He put his hat back on his head and trotted off.

Timothy let out a long breath.

Chapter 22

Kat's Justice

KAT SAT ON the front porch and stared into the murky, now cold contents of her father's abandoned coffee mug. Where was he? She went through a mental list of all the possible patients he might have been in a hurry to see. Nobody was in any current crisis as far as she knew. She swirled the cup's contents and threw the liquid onto the rose bush. At that moment she noticed that there were buds just days from bursting out in color, and with that awareness came the memory that she'd doubted she would stay this long.

Watch your back.

If there had been another robbery attempt, perhaps someone else had been shot. Could it have been that they didn't want to risk moving the injured man? And what if the injured man was one of the outlaws? Would they dare to ask her father to go to him? Would he have willingly gone with them?

I can't just sit here and wait for news. I can't! With no further delay, she pulled the Browning from the wall, picked up a box of ammunition from the cabinet and walked out of the house. Blue rolled her eyes warily at her while Kat pulled the saddle from its rack on the wall. In ten minutes, she was in the saddle, the rifle secured in the leather scabbard. She nudged Blue's sides and headed down the road to town for answers

Her boots rapped out staccato beats as she jogged up the steps of Gilford Hall's two-story house at the end of the street. She pounded on the door. For several minutes there was no response, and then she heard the sound of footsteps tapping across the wood floor. The door opened and Kat was looking into the face of a middle-aged Indian woman. She gave Kat a mild smile and asked what she wanted.

When the woman told her that Hall and another man had left just a little while ago, Kat spun on her heel and pulled herself into the saddle again. She knew where to look now. She felt the puzzle pieces were at last falling into place. She hoped she was wrong, but she knew in her heart that she wasn't.

She kicked Blue harder than necessary, causing the Morgan to leap forward into a run. Jonathan had said that if she needed him, to find him. She'd try the ranch, but if he wasn't there, she'd go on alone.

"That's exactly what he said." Timothy sat at the kitchen table, his head in his hands. "I'm no fighter, Jonathan. My boy means too much to me." He looked up, fear etching his face. "Jonathan, you've got to stop this man. You were a lawman, for God's sake."

Jonathan shook his head. "This isn't my job, Timothy. It isn't even my jurisdiction. I won't confront the man, but I'll protect those I care about. You and Adam number in that."

He didn't want to be right about this, but it was all turning out so predictably, like one continuous nightmare. Jonathan hadn't moved beyond the doorway. While looking at Timothy, his mind was already trying to think two moves ahead of the game players, or at least one.

"Timothy, I want you to go into town with Adam. Check into the boarding house. Don't leave the place until I come to you, and if I don't come to you in a day or two, light out to Smith's Ferry and try to get word to a U.S. Marshall." His voice was low and calm, almost as if suggesting they go on a holiday.

Timothy looked up, eyes wide. He opened his mouth to ask. . .*what*? *Is it really that bad? What about you? Why haven't you acted before now? Who is going to die this time?*

"Get moving!" Jonathan barked before Timothy could voice his thoughts. He didn't want to try and explain anything. There just wasn't time.

Timothy knocked his chair over in his haste to obey. Before he could strap on his own pistol and head for the door, Jonathan was gone.

If they were trying to cover their tracks, Kat and her father were going to be in someone's crosshairs. He had to get to her first.

Gilford Hall and Cahill rode into the clearing and found Nathaniel sitting casually on the porch with Ethan lying beside him. Nathaniel might have been just coming for a visit the way he sat relaxed with his back against the sagging porch post.

"Hello Gilford," Nathaniel said.

"Hello Nathaniel."

Gilford Hall scanned the clearing, looking first at the body of Liam and then coming to rest on his son. "How's my boy?"

"He's lost a lot of blood. Noah didn't know what to do. For some reason, he was afraid you'd kill him. That seems an odd thing, don't you think?" Nathaniel asked.

Hall seemed in no rush to get to his son's side, instead he remained seated on his horse like some manor Lord inspecting his kingdom. "It's an unfortunate situation we find ourselves in," he said.

"Only if you make it one," Nathaniel said matter-of-factly.

"Now how do you come to think that?"

"Well, you can do the smart thing or you can do the foolish thing." Nathaniel rubbed the back of his neck.

"I'll bite. What do you think that would be?" The elder Hall leaned forward, his elbow resting on the saddle horn.

"You could see that there are folks here who are onto what you've been up to. It may be a U.S. Marshall they bring in from Salt Lake, or it might be someone who'll finally get fed up and take a shot at you when you're sitting on your front porch, drinking a cup of coffee. You could see that probability, and you could take what you have and leave the Territory."

Hall's face was stone, his voice steel. "And I suppose that the foolish thing would be for me to kill you and your daughter and stay right where I am."

Nathaniel hoped his face did not reflect the sudden rush of fear for his daughter. He managed to answer flatly. "That about sums it up."

Hall straightened, giving him an unsafe smile. "I think you overestimate the backbone of our little town."

"He's right, Dad." Ethan's voice was soft and the words came out with obvious effort.

All eyes turned to Ethan, propped on one elbow, deathly pale.

"They know, and if they didn't before, they will now. You can't fight the whole town, Dad. Get out now, while you can."

"You don't look like you're in any condition to go anywhere," Hall said coldly.

"I don't plan to. If I pull through, I'll take my chances here and accept whatever they decide to do with me. I'm done with this." Ethan took a ragged breath. "I'm done with you."

Nathaniel never saw it coming, and neither did Ethan. Cahill had come up behind Nathaniel and pulled his hands behind him. In a minute he was trussed up like a pig.

Hall looked down at his son, his face contorted with a sneer. "*I'm* not the one going anywhere."

Jonathan pulled his bay to a sliding stop. He jumped down letting the reins remain looped on the saddle horn and ran to Kat's house. He called for her, and hearing no response he checked the barn for Blue. Surely, she wouldn't go out on her own. His memory pulled up the picture of her standing straight with the Browning rifle to her shoulder blasting away with deadly accuracy at those targets yesterday, and he knew with certainty that she would.

Running back to the house, he threw open the door. The Browning was gone from its rack on the wall. He whirled on his heel and ran for Jessie. His second-best skill as a Ranger had been as a tracker. He'd find her. He had to.

Kat slowed Blue as they approached the Hindricks' ranch house. There was an eerie, deserted cloud about the place. She walked to the door searching the yard and paddocks as she did, but only the mules stood there looking sleepy and bored. After knocking on the door and receiving no response, she called out. Trying the latch, she found that the door was unlocked. Inside the kitchen she found the remnants of an unfinished meal, the fallen chair, and puzzled over where they would have gone in a such a hurry.

Back on the porch, she cast her eyes to the hills bordering the small valley. The one place close enough to town and the wagon road that might provide the kind of privacy needed to hide the thieves and their stolen gold, would be there. That would explain the signs of use about the old trapper's cabin. And if Liam were involved, as she suspected, that would explain why she'd met him heading up the trail as she was returning home.

She knew she could be completely wrong, and she prayed she was, but her intuition screamed at her that her father was in grave danger. There was no time to wait for Jonathan. Without further hesitation, she mounted Blue, turning her head to the mountain.

Kat didn't want to take the beaten trail winding up to the cabin if the men were there. She wanted the element of surprise in her bag of ammunition. Requiring a little more time, she felt certain she could pick her way up the rockier side of the mountain. That would spill her out onto the far side of the cabin, and they wouldn't be expecting anyone to be foolish enough to risk the more dangerous approach.

Kat allowed Blue to blaze her own trail through a crowded stand of aspen. But when the pines closed in making riding impossible, she slipped down from the saddle, loosely tethering Blue to a bush. The little morgan protested her decision with no small amount of head throwing and pawing of ground.

"It's okay, Blue. I'll be back for you." She shuddered to think she might not be able to keep her promise.

Pulling her father's rifle from its scabbard, she checked the chamber, satisfied that it was loaded. She recalled wondering why her father had felt the need to purchase the newest edition, but now she was grateful that he had. If she and her father were going to walk away from this, she'd need every advantage.

Brush and low limbs pulled at her pant legs for a few hundred yards, making progress maddeningly slow. Then the vegetation suddenly changed to more sparsely scattered cedars, allowing her to make better time. Another quarter mile brought her to an open vista to the river, winding its snakelike path to Snowberry. From here, she'd need to pick her way carefully across the rocky face of the mountain.

Scanning the steep talus slope, she was dismayed to find only a narrow stony shoulder that might provide sure footing for the climb. She guessed that the rim was not much more than two hundred feet above where she stood. It wasn't like she hadn't done this kind of thing many times before, but she had been younger and immortal then. Years in surgery classes stitching broken bodies had shown her just how frail the human body actually was, including her own. Aside from the obvious danger of slipping to her death down the face of the mountain, there was the urgency to scale the rock quickly. She still didn't know how long her father had been gone. Seconds mattered.

Balancing the rifle on her shoulder seemed to help, shifting some of its weight to the middle of her body. With slow, careful steps she tested her footing on the slabs of stone. Gratefully, she realized that this face had not experienced any recent rock slides, so roots and projections of rock assisted her as she climbed. When she was what she estimated to be fifty feet from the rim, she stopped, catching her breath. Sweat trickled down her back. Her heart beat loudly in her ears.

Shifting the rifle to her other shoulder, she started again, finding the rock shelf easier to cross. Only a few feet from the top, she paused again, listening. Worrying that she had misjudged the proximity of the cabin to this side of the mountain, she hoped to hear voices. Keeping her head low she pulled herself the final few feet up onto the rim. Thickly spaced pines stood only a few feet from the cliff face. Slow quiet steps across a carpet of needles brought her to a place where she could see sunlight beyond the dense woodland.

She was still well back in the woods when she heard voices. Inching forward, she threaded her way through the trees in a crouched and ready position. It would do her father no good if she were taken as a second hostage. Ahead, light gleamed in an open clearing. The cabin stood just across the grassy field.

From here she'd have a clear view of the front of the cabin and the field. Kat knelt behind the tree and peered out into the field. Still exhausted from the climb, she rested her head against the tree, letting her heart slow, allowing her mind time to consider her options.

One man was sitting on his horse to the right of the cabin porch, another was crouched on the opposite side. With his back to her, was a younger man that looked like one of Liam's old crowd, a slow-thinking boy she'd known as Noah. Farther away, on the shaded porch, she could make out the slouched figure of a man, his back resting against the wall of the cabin.

Kat pulled back, rubbing sweat from her eyes with her free hand. She peered out from behind the tree again, straining to get a better look at the men. The man on the horse turned his head, giving her a chance to recognize him. Gilford Hall. The man who had been kneeling a few yards away turned as well. She assumed he was the man her father called Cahill, Hall's newest hired gun. She'd been right about the man closest to her. When he spoke to Hall, she recognized Noah's voice.

That was when she saw the crumpled form of a man at Noah's feet. It was impossible to see who he was from the position of his body with his face turned away, toward the cabin, but this wasn't her father. The clothes and body shape were wrong.

Shifting her eyes back to the porch she could make out the color of the man's hair who sat slumped there. She took in a sharp breath. It was Ethan Hall and even from here she could see the red stain on his shirt and the bandage. The bandage! Her father would have done that. Noah moved just a step to the left, allowing her to see her father, his hands tied to the porch post. Kat pulled herself back to the shelter of the tree, taking deep breaths to slow her heart. *Oh, Lord, if you're really there, I could sure use some help about now.*

Pressing her head back against the rough bark, she closed her eyes. She needed a plan. She always worked from a plan, a carefully thought out, *logical* plan. The best results were to follow prescribed treatment *plans*! But there wasn't time for that. No time for consulting books or even logic in this. This required strength of mind as much as body. And it required decisive action.

Rising from the ground she stepped into the field. Taking three quick, silent steps into the grass she raised the rifle to her shoulder. Gilford Hall was clearly in her sights and well in range.

"Drop your guns or I shoot your boss." Her gun was clearly leveled at Gilford Hall. All eyes turned to her in varying degrees of shock.

"I said *drop your guns*!"

From her left, out of the corner of her eye, she detected the shaking hands of Noah rising above his head. "Don't shoot, Miss Kat. I don't have my gun on me no more."

Noah had backed up a yard, now blocking her view of Cahill. "Noah! Get down!"

Cahill was bringing his rifle to bear on her. She saw him and swung her rifle in his direction, firing just as Noah dropped to the ground. She quickly chambered another round, swinging the rifle back to the elder Hall. The horse was there but Hall was gone. Frantically, she scanned the area, the gun still to her shoulder. Lifting her head from the sights, she saw Cahill on the ground, groaning. His rifle lay beside him where he'd dropped it, while Noah remained huddled on the ground to her left.

She stepped beside him and glanced down to assure herself that he didn't have a gun. Then she saw the face of the dead man beside him. It was Liam, face gray with death.

Continuing to scan the area for Hall, she hissed to Noah, "Noah, I need you to help me. Go over to that man and kick his gun as far from him as you can." When all she got back from him was whimpering, she asked in a tone that left no room for argument, "Are you willing to do that, Noah?"

"Yes, Miss Kat," he sobbed stumbling to his feet. Crossing the field at a run, he kicked the gun before running in the direction of the paddock. Lifting her head from her sights, she saw him pull his horse loose from the rail and swing up onto his back. There was no reason to stop him. He'd be one less threat. She had enough to worry about here with Hall still somewhere and in a fine position to ambush her.

At the moment Noah galloped past her and down the trail, a familiar voice cried out to her from the right. "Kat! Look out! Beside the house, to your right!"

She saw the man, gun in hand bringing it up to bear on her. Kat ran for all she was worth in the direction of her father to the left, hoping to reach the shelter of the porch steps before he could fire. Her father sat completely helpless, hands tied behind his back. Running with her back bent, head down, she dove the final few feet toward the porch steps. A shot came thunderously out of the woods to her right. There was a cry that followed and a blur of movement at the corner of the house. Gilford Hall stumbled into view. Grabbing for the porch post, he dropped his gun. For a moment he held himself there. Before he slipped to the ground, Kat saw the surprise open his mouth one last time, but no words came.

Jonathan stepped from the woods, his rifle still to his shoulder, one eye on Kat and the other on Gilford Hall, the man he'd just shot. He continued to walk with slow deliberate steps in the direction of the house and Kat.

Kat scrambled to her feet, grabbing for her father's arm. "Are you all right? Did they hurt you?"

"I'm fine. Just a little bump on the head." He tipped his head toward Ethan. "Not sure about him."

Kat looked over at Ethan, who was sitting up, his face pale. "Hey, Dr. Kat. Glad you're all right." His voice was soft, his mouth drawn up into a half smile.

She rose to her feet, turning in his direction. Ethan's face contorted as he yelled out, "Look out!" She saw him reach for his pistol. Ethan managed to lift it pointing it in her direction. Confused, she dropped to the ground in front of the porch, dropping her rifle as she did. Two pistols exploded. Silence then. Lifting her head, she saw Ethan grab his arm and looking back over her shoulder she saw Cahill on his feet, with blood dripping from his hand where Ethan's bullet had hit him.

Her one thought was to get to her father before Cahill could. She stumbled over the porch step and fell by her father's side. Before she could regain her footing, a bloody arm had wrapped itself around her and pulled her to her feet. Cahill swung her around, her back now to the porch and her father, facing the field where Jonathan stood with the Winchester aimed at Cahill.

"Let her go. It's over." Jonathan's voice came soft but deadly.

Kat made an excellent shield for Cahill. The man's whiskered cheek scratched her scalp as he gripped her tightly to his chest. She could smell the sweat of fear on him, but his laugh revealed that he believed he had nothing to lose.

"I ain't so sure it's over," he growled. "I think I'm going to take this sweet little girl and ride out of here, and there won't be anything you can do about it." Kat felt the sharp prick of a knife pressing into her side.

Jonathan walked steadily across the field, the butt of his rifle still tight against his shoulder.

"That's far enough!" Cahill snarled.

"Let her go!" Jonathan's voice was steel. But Kat saw him pull his gaze from the rifle sights, and in those dark eyes she caught a glimpse of the horrors he'd lived with too long. She knew that her death would ruin him, and in a moment resolved that she would not become one more ghost to haunt his days and nights.

Kat could feel Cahill's blood, sticky and warm, soaking through the back of her shirt. With sudden realization she knew that it was flowing from the wound she'd inflicted. No plan, but an instinct for survival prompted her to ram her elbow back, sharply jabbing it into the area of the open wound. The man let out a heavy grunt, a second later his grip relaxed. Pulling herself free, she rolled to the left just as Jonathan took his shot, straight and sure to the man's chest. Cahill dropped the knife, lifting his hand to cover the hole. A second more passed before he fell face forward into the dirt.

Kat stumbled to her feet, looking wildly about her. And then Jonathan had her, holding her safe in his arms. At first, she struggled, imagining some other source of threat with a grip on her.

"It's all right," Jonathan said. "It's all right," he repeated, holding her more tightly to him.

She leaned her head against his heaving chest. A violent shiver, a final drain of adrenaline left her feeling weak.

Jonathan's fingers slid through her hair and held her there. Only for a moment did they stand there frozen in the aftermath, only a moment before Jonathan said softly, "You have a patient to attend to."

She looked up into his somber, gray eyes and saw him nod in the direction of the porch.

"He needs you. Go! I'll see to your Dad." He released her, walking quickly to her father.

Ethan's head drooped on his chest. Running up the steps, she knelt beside him. Seeing her father's bag a few feet away, she reached for it and pulled it to her. In her rush, she spilled some of its contents.

Taking air in great gulps, she tried to steady her hands to inspect the fresh wound on his shoulder. *It wasn't that bad,* she told herself, *through the flesh.* She could clean it and have him bandaged in a few minutes.

Ethan opened his eyes and lifted his head, turning his pale eyes to her face. "Hey, Dr. Kat. You goin' try and patch me up?" He laughed, a rasping sound that faded into a groan. "Don't you think it's too late for that?"

Kat rummaged frantically through the bag for clean cloths to staunch the flow of blood. There was so much of it. Her pants were soaking it up from the pool in which she knelt. Her medical training had taught her how much blood the body held, and as she stared down her head tried to calculate the percentage that was outside her patient's body, and how little was left inside. She looked up, her eyes welling with tears as she pressed the cloth firmly into the wound.

Ethan's lips were moving, but no sound came. She leaned in with her ear close to his lips.

"Wish I could've been a man as straight as that one," he breathed. He looked beyond her to where Jonathan knelt by Nathaniel's side. "Somewhere along the line I . . .got bent."

Kat touched his lips with her finger and shook her head. "Hush! Save your strength. I can help you."

She pressed the cloth harder against the hole in his shoulder, the blur of tears obscuring her sight. "I can fix this," she whispered.

"Kat, he's gone." Her father was by her side, his hands on hers.

She looked at her father, confused.

"He's gone, Kat. You can't help him anymore."

The words registered in her foggy brain and she looked down at the face of Ethan, his blue eyes open but sightless.

Firm hands gripped her shoulders from behind. Jonathan pulled her to her feet. Trembling, she turned to him, letting him enfold her in his arms again. She stood there with her arms limp at her sides, the blood-soaked cloths still gripped in her fingers.

Beyond where they stood, the bodies of three men lay sprawled in the dirt beyond the help of any physician. All of this had taken only minutes, deadly minutes that had claimed four lives. The adrenaline of the past hour suddenly spent, her knees buckled beneath her.

Jonathan did not let her fall, but gently eased her to the ground, where he knelt in the dirt with her body cradled in his arms. The warmth of him countered the sudden chill that had gripped her. She wrapped her arms around him, drawing him tightly to her.

"I couldn't save him, Jonathan." The words came choked. Hot tears flowed down her cheeks, soaking his shirt.

"No." He rested his chin on her head and spoke softly into her hair.

Kat looked up into Jonathan's face without asking the question.

Jonathan pulled her back to his chest. "But he made the choice of a good man."

Another spasm of trembling gripped her as she buried her face into Jonathan's arm. Gently stroking her hair, he rocked her in his arms as if she were a child.

Around him, Jonathan no longer saw the red that had colored his nightmares. Instead, he saw the colors of morning. The woman in his arms was warm with life coursing through her veins. Against his chest, he could feel her heart beating strong and steady. He was awake and somehow, he knew the nightmare would not return.

Jonathan whispered into her hair, "Dear Dr. Kat, you've saved us both."

Chapter 24

A Healer's Care

KAT BENT OVER the rosebush, taking in a deep breath of the first open blossom. She sighed as pleasant memories mingled with the sweet fragrance. Mama would have been pleased. With the deftness of a surgeon, she clipped the rose stem just above a branch with five leaves. She carried the rose back to the house and flopped down on the porch swing, burying her nose in the blossom.

Looking toward the west, she watched as the sun neared the summit of the range that bordered her peaceful valley. Pale hues of orange and pink were already brushing warm streaks across the jagged peaks and high valleys. She lay the rose on her lap and reached into her pocket, pulling out the tattered envelope along with the one she'd never mailed.

Snowberry's white-washed buildings glowed in softly painted colors of sunset. This was still her town. Looking down at the envelopes in her lap, she allowed herself a quiet smile. With the same quick, sure strokes she'd used to snip the rose stem she cut the envelopes into eight neat pieces. One at a time she pushed them into her pocket. It was time to write another letter, one that would close a door to a dream. But new dreams can replace the old. And Snowberry offered her enough to satisfy the need she had to use her gifts to heal and bring hope.

The sounds of hoof beats drew her eyes back to the road where Jessie was bringing Jonathan to dinner.

Jonathan slipped easily from the saddle and led Jessie to the barn. Jessie and Blue had a kind of understanding now, and at times could be convinced to share a portion of grass. It didn't hurt the relationship that Jonathan usually added a handful of grain to each portion.

Kat waited at the door to the barn for him to unsaddle the bay. Before closing the paddock gate, Jonathan gave his mare a pat on her rump. Kat reached out a hand to him and he took it with a smile creasing the corners of his eyes. He had a very nice smile, now that he had found it again.

"I'm glad you could come," Kat said.

"I never knew a Texan to turn down a good meal. Don't plan to be the first," Jonathan said in his deadpan Texas drawl.

"I don't think Papa is quite ready. We had two minor surgeries today." She pulled him toward the garden. "Come see the crabapple trees. They're just starting to bud."

The warm light of sunset projected long shadows across the lawn where they strolled, creating a lacework pattern that they interrupted with their passing.

Jonathan stopped halfway across the lawn. Kat turned, throwing him a quizzical expression.

"I told them I'd run," Jonathan said softly.

Kat's eyes widened. "Run for sheriff? But I thought..."

Jonathan laced her fingers through his, studying the contrast of her thin white ones against his rough calloused ones. "I know I did. But I'm just like you in many ways. You can't deny what you've been called to do any more than I can. You heal as you can. I. . . I protect as much as I'm able."

"Dear, Jonathan, you did." Kat withdrew her hand from his, drawing her fingers along his cheek. "You did protect. I'm not sure that I could have lived with the knowledge of taking a life."

For a moment, she thought he was going to kiss her. Instead, he stepped back and reached into his pocket, pulling out a flat metal object. Taking her hand again he held it in his, her palm up. Into her hand he placed the star of the Texas Rangers. She looked up into his face, her brow creased in question.

"I think you should keep it. You're the one who brought law back to this valley. On your own, you braced the sheriff. I just backed you up."

At first, she thought he might be teasing, but she saw the solemn expression on his face and knew no joke was intended.

Kat stood looking down at the star in her hand, her mouth slightly open. In a sense, she had taken the law into her own hands, but she felt no sense of satisfaction in it. It had come at too high a cost. Two weeks had passed since that deadly morning, and each move, each shot fired she recalled with picture clarity. But the question that remained unanswered was why Ethan had defended her. She certainly hadn't inspired his loyalty. Something else had been at work.

Her father's confession of asking a new type of question made her wonder if she too should be asking who instead of why, because her why questions were coming up empty. Something had happened up there in the high valley, something or someone had played a hand that had allowed all three of them to walk out unharmed.

Jonathan reached for her other hand, not seeing the rose she held.

"Ow!" Kat dropped the rose and looked at where the thorn had pierced her finger. A single crimson drop of blood formed on the tip. Jonathan took her hand, lifted the finger to his lips and kissed it.

Kat laughed lightly. "Do you know how many germs you just injected into my blood stream?"

Jonathan frowned and then shook his head before pulling her into his arms. "I guess I'm the romantic in this twosome." He lifted her chin with his finger. "You and me got a long road ahead to figure this out, because we're about as different as two people can be."

"I have to agree. But it's sure going to be fun getting there," she said with a teasing smile.

She looked up into his strange gray eyes and wrapped her arms around his neck. Pulling his head down to her, she kissed him. Lifting herself to her toes, she pressed her lips to his warm ones. At last, she released him, her mouth sliding up into a smile devoid of teasing. "I'm not sorry for that at all, not one bit."

Picking her up, holding her close to his chest, he kissed her again. This time she allowed herself to experience the intensity of her attraction to him, the tingling joy of his firm arms around her, the longing for more. She yielded because this was a good man, a straight man, a man worthy of the wait.

When he finally let her go, she stood before him breathless, but the words fell from her lips as surely as the petals of a rose in an irresistible summer wind. "I think I love you, Jonathan Winthrop."

Nathaniel Meriwether let out a low whistle. "Thought I'd never hear her say that."

They turned their heads in the direction of the voice.

"Supper's ready, that is, if you're interested," Nathaniel said before turning back to the house.

Jonathan traced her cheek with his finger, before lifting her chin and kissing her once again. This time it was a kiss filled with the passion of a man who knew what he wanted as much as what he needed. Before releasing her, Jonathan brushed the top of her head with his lips. Leaning in close to her ear, he whispered, "I can't help but love you too, dear Kat."

His soft breath on her neck sent delightful shivers down her back. Pulling him close, she lay her head on his chest while he stroked her hair. The pounding of his heart matched hers perfectly, and she was as content as she had ever been in her life. In his arms and in his heart, she knew she was safe and she would stay.

Kat's healing work had already begun to have its effect on Jonathan. Dreams had replaced the nightmare, dreams of a girl with chestnut hair and large brown eyes who could handle a rifle nearly as capably as a scalpel. A woman who valued justice as much as he. Hope had taken root that springs up alongside the lupine and wild roses bordering the wide river. In time and with a healer's care, the wound would heal. Hope would blossom and bear fruit.

With hands entwined, they followed Nathaniel, taking their time while sunset colors bathed the path in soft light. When they stepped up onto the porch, Nathaniel was waiting by the door, a lopsided grin stretching from one ear to the other. With his thumb, he pointed to the newly hung sign to the right of the door. "What do 'ya think, little girl?"

Dr. Kathryn Meriwether

&

Dr. Nathaniel Meriwether

Kat's face opened into a wide confident smile. "Looks perfect, Papa, just perfect!"

Other Books in the Sawtooth Range Series

High Valley Promise

Comes the Winter

Redeeming Lies

A Portrait of Dawn

I love hearing from readers. You can connect with me on my website. www.samanthastclaire.com

www.ingramcontent.com/pod-product-compliance
Lightning Source LLC
Chambersburg PA
CBHW021118110726

47900CB00007B/2235